the Three Feathers

To Ethan,

May the chosen
be with you, always.

[signature]

Stefan Bolz

～

The Three Feathers

STEFAN BOLZ

ISBN-13:978-0615648750

Beacon Books Publishing

Cover by Matt Maley

Interior Book Design by Donnie Light

Table of Contents

1. Dreams 1

2. Death 6

3. Departure 10

4. Wolf...13

5. Krieg...20

6. Water 28

7. Wind 40

8. Jump 46

9. Eagles 56

10. Mirrors...63

11. Ruins..78

12. Refuge 91

13. Lioness 100

14. Darkness 111

15. Alda 114

16. Capture 125

17. Broga 133

18. Submerged...142

19. Ambushed..155

20. Awakening 166

21. The Long Dark 170

22. Battle 178

23. Dragon's Flight 191

24. Home 202

25. Epilogue 211

The Journey on the Map...212

About the Author...214

Thank You

hank you, Layla Mosbacher, for being my first beta reader for a lot of the scenes. Thank you for your encouragement and your enthusiasm for the story. Now I know why your middle name is Hope. Thank you, Chloe Mosbacher, for filling the writing space with the smell of brownies, fudge, and almond extract. Because of you I might have a permanent association between cookies and the story. Thank you, Amy Mosbacher, for listening to countless hours of me talking about the story and you telling me each time—and however strange an idea was—that it was great.

Many thanks to Mrs. Coogan and her 4th grade class at Lenape Elementary School in New Paltz, NY, for having one of the manuscript copies read aloud in class. That was amazing. Thanks to Elke Kaeppner, Diane Silverberg ("I'm the rooster! I'm the rooster!"), Mercedes Calderon, Julie Rose, Gerald Sorin, Jed Sherman, Maxine & Marielle Rosola, Julie Nichols, Carla Aiston (a.k.a. frog princess), Lynn Masanotti (Lynn, I completely understand that you had to finish *50 Shades of Gray* first. No hard feelings), Jackie Dooley and Laura Putnam, for reading the first draft and giving invaluable feedback. Thank you, Maxi Spanheimer, for being who you are, always. Thank you (again) Jackie Dooley for editing the manuscript in your 'free time'. Thanks, Matt Maley at Visualstuff in New Paltz, for an amazing and inspired cover. Thanks to Donnie Light from eBook76.com for making the pages look beautiful.

Thanks to all my early Facebook page likers. Your out-pour of support was touching and bridged the gap over some chasms I had to cross in order to get to the other side. Thank you, Julie Lion Rose, for letting me play in the sand box at your therapy practice and thereby—and because of it—conceive Joshua's story and everything that followed. Thank you Joyce Urritia for your understated brilliance in Astrology and your side statement of: "Oh, and, by the way, you should go back to therapy and please for God's sake STOP EDITING YOURSELF!" Wow, that was a good one.

Thanks to my family and friends in Germany. You are with me far across the ocean. I am forgetting people to thank, I'm sure. Just know that you are not forgotten.

Finally, thank you so much, Joshua, for letting me be your scribe; for choosing me to write it all down. Thank you, Grey and Krieg, for your undying friendship. I feel honored for the privilege of being part of your journey. Thank you Alda, for your music; Wind for your wisdom and warmth; Dragon-of-the-Stone for sharing your magnificent dreams; Broga for your might & confidence; and you, lioness, for your stunning beauty and grace. I dare sometimes to summon you and you are there each time I do.

New York in August 2012,

Stefan Bolz

"The goal of the journey is neither the journey itself nor its end. It is but the companions we collect on the way."

– Joshua Aylong

For You

1. *Dreams*

O nce upon a time there was a rooster who lived on a farm on the eastern shore somewhere between the Tundra-like highlands to the south and the lush low grasslands of the north. His name was Joshua Aylong. Joshua led a comfortable life watching over the hens in his coop, protecting them from predators and announcing each new day at precisely 4:45 AM. His feathers were red as the sun rising over the mountains; a deep red on top and a more orange color toward his chest. His tail feathers had a bluish hue to it which gave him the appearance, depending on where the sun hit them, of a tropical bird rather than a rooster. The hens loved him for his striking colors and he, being a somewhat smart and self aware bird, knew it and loved every minute of it, basking in the attention. You could see him more often than not walk around inside the pen, his head held high, strutting his stuff among the hens and chicks of his flock.

But at night when all was still, when the busy pecking and roosting and strutting around quieted down, when the last rays of sunlight disappeared behind the Great Lake to the east, Joshua felt a longing inside him, a longing he could neither explain nor talk about nor even fully grasp. It was just there whenever the noises of the day ebbed down to stillness; when the rustling and bustling inside the coop stopped and all was quiet. The longing was like a pull or perhaps a push at times but he experienced it more like a pull. From where he did not know. It dawned on him one night, somewhere between midnight and 2AM when all he could hear was the distant waves breaking onto the shore in the moonlit night—it dawned on him that he was looking for something. Something bigger. Something wider. Something …vast. Something more than what was in front of him each day and every day after that day.

At that moment, when the moon stood high over the darkened hills and the silhouettes of the other chickens in the coop were all black against the window, he decided that he had to go and find whatever it was he was looking for. It all seemed very clear to him. He thought he would just stand on the highest perch inside the pen, spread his wings and in a combination of jumping and pushing his wings down hard several times he would fly out of the pen and land on the other side. From there he would just walk.

But two minutes and twelve second after he first had the thought of leaving, he became distracted by a noise from outside the coop and he forgot all about it and, suddenly tired, he fell into a dreamless sleep from which he woke at 4:44 AM, like clockwork, to call out the next day.

Nothing noteworthy happened over the next few months, at least nothing that was a departure from the daily routine. Joshua had forgotten all about that clear and cloudless night and his decision to begin his journey. Only once in a while, sometimes while picking for food or settling a quarrel between some of the hens or while strutting around in the pen showing off his colors, you could watch him stop suddenly as if trying to grasp a distant thought, a fleeting feeling or a trace of memory from somewhere. Then it was gone and he continued with whatever it was he was doing at that moment. Until the dreams began.

They were foggy at first, indistinct and you could barely call them dreams. More like mysterious clouds that were solid only on the edges. But over time an image carved itself out of the fog like a figure sculpted from clay by invisible hands. Joshua began to see what looked like an immense cave. The massive walls of it extended for miles in all directions and one could only see the lower parts of them going upward toward the ceiling that was in itself invisible and lay in mystery and nothingness. As he walked, all by himself in the vast cave feeling the ever changing ground under his talons—from areas of very fine, almost white sand to large plates of flat rock covered with silvery gray moss— he seemed to move toward a certain point far in the distance. Each time he tried to focus on what it was he was looking at, he woke up. Each night he tried anew and in time he was able to get closer and closer to the shape in the distance. He began to think about the dream during the day and the hens in the pen began to talk among themselves about his absent mindedness and his, at times, lack of focus on what he was doing. Once during an especially vivid dream he thought he saw a large feather in the distance but the image faded almost instantly, leaving him wanting it even more.

During this time he started to peck at the other hens more frequently and more harshly than he intended to, not knowing where this sudden increase in frustration came from. His daily tasks meant less and less to him and the joys he usually experienced during the day faded and were soon exchanged for a sense of hopelessness and despair. "What's the use," he thought more often than not. The hens swore that the colors of his feather coat became less brilliant during that time and his proud and at times almost charismatic presence lessened to the point of non existence. He wanted for the dream to stop. He wanted to just be left alone rather than wander every night endlessly through the vastness of the cave moving slowly toward something in the distance that seemed to stay out of reach forever. Sometimes during the dream he thought he should turn around or go in another direction but there didn't seem to be another place in the tremendous cave that felt like there was something of value except in the one direction he was going toward.

At some point he reached a river. Its slow-flowing water was crystal clear and of deep turquoise. He walked beside it for a while. One night he dreamed that he would just sit down next to it and die right there. Let go of his feathers, his flesh and skin and bones. Let go of his memories and thoughts and all that he was. But as hard as he tried it didn't work and, even though he felt more dead than alive, he didn't seem to be able to give up completely.

And then, one night in deepest winter, after fresh snow had fallen onto the hills above the farm and the land below and the cold crept into the coop like large tongs of frozen ice, the image in his dream suddenly became clear. He knew he was still a distance away but he could make out the cave wall more clearly. He saw that what he at first thought was just a lighter coloring on the wall, was actually a smaller cave adjacent to this one whose ceiling emitted a slight glow as if there was, behind the thick walls, a massive source of light. As he drew nearer, he saw that the light made the walls nearly transparent and, in looking even closer, Joshua saw small threads going through the transparent crystalline stone like veins. The steady glow illuminated the cave just enough to see what was inside.

When he entered the small cave, small only in relation to the vastness of the larger one, he was stunned by the beauty of the patterns in the walls and ceiling. The vein-like threads were like rivers in the earth observed from high above. There were small indentations of darker color shimmering in shades of blue that looked like large bodies of water, deep crevasses changed to mountain ranges interspersed with green and aventurine patches that looked like pastures. He felt the strange sensation of looking down on an incredibly detailed, magnificent landscape rather than looking up toward a ceiling of stone. Joshua briefly experienced vertigo until he adjusted to the upside down view. He had never seen anything like it and in no imagination or past dream had he ever seen such beauty.

And then his gaze followed the turquoise shimmer of what looked like a great river, down toward where the ceiling met the floor. There stood a cylindrical stone, deep black and smooth like polished quartz. At its top lay three feathers. When he looked at them closely, they seemed to change their colors, first reflecting his own palette, and moving through the spectrum of the rainbow from deepest green to yellow and blue. He could not keep his eyes off them. He thought them to be the most precious things in all the universe and it was then, while he dreamed, that he experienced for the first time what it meant to be fully loved. It overwhelmed him and he woke.

It was still dark in the coop. As he looked at the hens on their perches in front and beside him, the intense feeling of love he had felt in his dream spilled out from him and into the coop and for an instant longer Joshua loved all of the hens with the same all encompassing love. He even loved the perches themselves, the walls of the coop, the hay-covered floor, the window and the night beyond. There was no being that was not enveloped in his love. For a short moment longer he felt that it encompassed him completely and then, like a shooting star disappearing in the night sky, the feeling lingered a moment longer and dissipated. It left him empty, cold, and lonelier than he had ever felt before. The warm bodies of the other chickens in the coop could not give him warmth or company or help him close the wound in his soul. He was alone.

2. Death

he days and weeks that followed were nothing but grayness—gray days, dark nights and a chill wind from the sea that wouldn't let up. The snow that remained was brown and iced over. The food had a stale taste to it. And while the hens and half-grown chicks were busy scratching the patches of grass and dirt looking for worms, Joshua just glanced at them impatiently, disturbing their peace whenever he could. He was jealous of their content lives. For them it was all about finding food and water, scratching the soil and laying eggs. He could not find any satisfaction in it anymore. He was overcome by a sense of restlessness during the day and sleeplessness by night. As much as he wished to go back to the dream, he could not find a way there. It eluded him to the extent that he tried to day dream to bring the images back into his mind—the images of the three feathers on the black cylinder of stone.

He increasingly saw the coop as a prison rather than a safe haven and a home. He found himself gazing longingly through the fence and toward the world beyond. "I need to find them," he thought to himself one day. "I have to find them." Joshua could feel the unrest among the hens when he jumped up onto the highest perch of the pen. For a moment he thought he should just stay with them, protect them, settle their quarrels, and strut his stuff in front of them as he always did. But something inside him knew that he would not be able to do that anymore. And when this something, this force inside him, swelled up and grew and became utterly unbearable, he opened his wings and jumped.

It took him several flaps to reach the height of the fence. At the last moment he almost didn't make it but he pushed and put everything he had into his final flap. Then he was past the fence and landed on the other side. The hens came toward him, wanting to follow him, but couldn't understand that there was now a barrier between them. He was unreachable. He was free. A rush of excitement filled him as he walked away from the fence. One more time he looked back, pushing down the feeling of regret. Then he turned his head and concentrated on the task before him.

Joshua didn't have the slightest idea where to go but he thought that he would cross the large meadow first and find shelter under the trees in the thick woods beyond. The other direction was water and he did not want to walk along the beach, out of fear of being too exposed. As he stood at the edge of the meadow looking far across to the other side he suddenly wasn't so sure anymore. Did he really just fly out of the pen and leave his home, the place where he was born and grew up in; the place where he had lived all his life? It seemed silly all of a sudden. Why did he do this? He couldn't find any logical explanation for it. For a moment he was torn. Maybe he should just go back. Maybe this wasn't such a good idea after all. But as he was here now, he thought that he might as well see what's on the other side of the field. He could always come back.

And so he began to cross the large meadow. This was much easier said than done. The snow was iced over at points and large patches of the grass were still frozen and stood out like huge spikes from the ground. After he was halfway across, he realized that the sun was way past the midpoint and that in a few hours it would be dark. He wanted to make it to the edge of the woods before nightfall and find shelter in one of the trees. By now, he was convinced that he would return to his flock the next morning. And then he heard it.

It was a low cry, distant at first, but moving closer fast. Joshua dropped to the ground. He realized that his red feathered coat made him visible against the white snow and the green and brown grass. When he saw the owl—its wing span three times his own, her talons double the size of his and a beak that could break his legs in one bite, he felt as if death itself came for him. He lay frozen on the ground not breathing and almost trying to make his heart stop out of fear of being detected. When he turned his head slightly he saw her, gracefully gliding against the sky, circling overhead. He was sure she was about to come for him any second, diving down and grabbing him, lifting him up into the air to take him to a spot where she could start eating him only to leave the head and feathers behind when she was done. But to his surprise she didn't come toward him. Instead he followed her flight path with his eyes until the realization hit him full force: the pen! Now unprotected, the hens had no warning. The owl would have easy prey. She could effortlessly kill three or four birds before the rest would be able to flee under the coop.

Joshua had always warned the hens about birds of prey. He had seen the owl several times way before any of the hens would have even been aware. Once he spotted a hawk. When he had seen him approach, not more than a spec before the low sun, he cried out and the hens jumped under the coop to safety just in time.

He knew from the moment he saw the owl's flight path that it would be too late. He cried out as loud as he could and jumped and ran toward the barn. There was no way he would be there in time to warn them. He flew when he could, stumbled several times and once even crashed head first into a snow drift. Time seemed to thicken like syrup and Joshua thought it an eternity before he finally reached the pen. What he saw there was an image of horror. There were feathers everywhere. Two hens and a younger chick lay dead on the ground inside the pen. He frantically tried to get inside but to no avail. There was no jumping off point to get high enough to fly in. He circled the pen trying to see who was left. He saw some commotion under the coop but he couldn't see anything under there.

"I should have stayed," he thought to himself. "I should have watched over them." The thoughts had, at first, barely any emotion connected to them. He just very rationally realized his part in the death of his flock. He felt removed from himself as if outside looking in on the scene in front of him.

"You left us," one of the hens looked at him from under the coop. "You were supposed to protect us and you left. This is your fault."

"I'm sorry," Joshua replied. "I'm so sorry. I didn't mean to... I didn't know..."

A second hen looked at him. "What are you still doing here? You left us. Go. Leave! There's no place for you here anymore." And with that she turned away from him and went back under the coop. The other hen looked at him for a moment longer, then turned and disappeared as well.

He stood there, grasping on the periphery that his life as he had known it until now, was over. "I'm sorry about what happened," he thought to himself. "I'm so sorry." As if waiting for an answer he looked at the place where the two hens had just stood. Maybe they would come out again, look at him and tell him that it was okay, that it wasn't his fault and that he could come back into the pen and continue to live with them. But they didn't come.

3. Departure

The chill easterly wind from the bay ruffled his feathers. He didn't know why he stayed at the spot where he had spoken to the hens, but he did. It felt hard for him to move. "I can just sit here for a while," he thought. "See what happens." He sat and watched the coop for any movement from the hens. As the sun began to set over the hills, the lights in the farm house came on. Then the door opened and the farmer stepped outside. He came straight toward the pen, not paying any attention to Joshua. When he saw what had happened, the farmer cried out. His face red from anger, he cursed at the sky while he collected the limp bodies of the dead chickens. When he came out of the pen he went straight toward Joshua. He dropped the chickens to the ground and tried to grab him while still cursing and yelling. The farmer's large callused hands almost caught Joshua twice, once grabbing one of his wings. He eluded him but barely. In the end, the farmer kicked at him until Joshua escaped into a nearby tree. From there he watched the farmer eventually collecting the dead chickens and walking off toward the house.

He stayed all night on his branch high up in the tree. His dreams were dark and filled with the small and lifeless bodies of his flock. The two hens cursed him over and over, their eyes dead and their feathers bloody. Several times he awoke in the dark, wishing himself back inside the soft warmth of the coop and the small rustling sounds and familiar features of the others. He could not yet fully grasp that this part of his life was irrevocably over, gone like fog in summer's sun, erased and not belonging to him anymore.

At first light, when everything was still quiet except for the wind in the tree tops above, he flew down from his branch and made his way to the meadow. He did not look back. Several times he thought he had to, but he stopped himself each time.

"The sooner I forget, the better," he told himself. As he began to cross the meadow for the second time, a cold, steady rain set in, soaking his feathers down to his skin. There was no tree to stand under, no bush to find refuge in. The openness of the seemingly endless field was unsettling. Joshua caught himself looking in all directions many times over, spotting creatures where there were only shadows. He saw a fox in the shape of a distant snow drift, a raccoon in a patch of grass that seemed to move in his direction. His eyes played tricks on him until he thought to himself that there was no use in even thinking this way. If any predator wanted to eat him, there was nothing he could do about it.

When he finally reached the trees, he was exhausted, hungry and needed water badly. His left talon started to hurt him and he needed a place to rest and eat something really soon. Under a large oak tree he found a couple of worms who had made their way out of the ground during the rain. A small trickle of a stream provided water. He was hoping to come across a large pine tree to find refuge for the night but none of the trees had leaves on them. So he spent the night on a slippery branch in the rain, his body close to the stem of the tree for protection from the wind. He did not want to miss his flock but he did. He missed them all terribly—the ones that were dead, the ones who still lived, and even the hens that had cursed him.

The next few days passed in a haze for Joshua as he made his way through the forest. The rain stopped for a while, then continued on and off. The cold was his constant companion and except for one night, where he slept in the remnants of an old fallen down barn that smelled like mice and induced the terror of a fox coming for him, he slept in the rain, somewhere high up in a tree out of reach for at least some of the predators. His thoughts circled around his flock and the horrible mistake he had made in leaving them. There was no place for him to go and he saw the remainder of his life before him, extending into infinity in an endless spiral of regret. This wasn't what he had in mind.

In the evening of the third day, Joshua saw a patch of blue sky through the trees and, as he reached the edge of the forest, he watched the sun set in the eastern sky, flooding the land before him with golden light. But even as he stood there gazing at the horizon and the gloriously beautiful painted sky over the valley, he could not find peace. He was sure it would elude him until he died.

4. Wolf

*T*he next morning, Joshua arose at exactly 4:44 AM and without even thinking, he crowed his wake up call until he realized there was nobody to wake up. He sat on his branch high in the tree and wished himself back into the coop until bits and pieces of last night's dream came back to him—a dream of feathers so fragile that when he touched them they crumpled until what was left of them was only dust. Of the glorious dream he had, before he decided to make this journey, only a distorted image stayed with him, not reminiscent of the original powerful vision but merely an after image. And he began to question even that. "I'll never make it," he thought to himself. "I'll probably get lost somewhere in the wilderness until I finally become just another meal for a fox."

As the light increased, a blanket of thick layered fog appeared, resting in the valley before him. As Joshua followed the fog with his eyes all the way to the other side of the valley, he saw the peak of a high mountain towering above the fog. For the smallest of moments, the shape of the mountain stirred deep inside him the memory of the dream. He thought briefly that he had seen it in his dream somewhere in the cave's ceiling. He knew suddenly and unmistakably where he had to go. His eyes fixed on the snow covered peak in the distance. Somewhere beneath it lay the three feathers waiting for him in the dim shadows of the massive cave. And perhaps his own redemption lay there as well.

As he made his way through the fog, going from boulder to boulder for cover and glancing in all directions, he heard a howl in the distance. At First it was far away, but as he moved it got closer. Always to his left, it seemed to hold his own speed. When evening came, Joshua took refuge halfway up a large boulder in a small crevasse. He could not find sleep that night. And when he did, he dreamed that he stood in front of a black hole, frozen in terror. Red eyes peered at him from within the darkness. He couldn't move, as if his body didn't belong to him. He tried to scream but no sound escaped his beak. There was a gray shadow coming toward him with immense speed and just before it reached him, he awoke. Joshua realized that there probably would be no moment during his journey when he would be completely safe.

The next day the fog was gone as if it never happened in the first place. Far across the valley—much further than Joshua thought when he saw it first—stood the snow covered mountain in the distance. Joshua tried to hold it in his line of sight as he navigated his way through the high grass of the frozen fields. Once in a while he fluttered up in the air to get a better look, fully aware that he was exposing himself to everything and everyone around him. When the sun set behind the mountain he realized that he badly needed water.

Maybe it was because he was getting tired from the constant jumping up and hopping through the grass when suddenly, after yet another jump, Joshua landed right in front of a hole in the ground. It didn't register at first. But when he saw the grass around the opening pushed flat into a path leading away from it, he realized in terror that he stood in front of a fox hole.

He froze. Unable to move, Joshua stared into the hole. The small feathers around his neck stood up. He thought it a hallucination at first when two red eyes appeared inside the blackness, staring at him. Never had he seen anything more frightening in his life. He was suddenly certain of his death. Slowly, the eyes came closer until the fox's head appeared. What occurred next happened so fast he wasn't sure of the exact sequence of it. He heard a sound on his left, like a fast movement through the grass. The fox, low to the ground, came out of his hole and, without any warning, jumped toward Joshua who, at the same time, flew up in the air. He saw the fox land where he had been standing. While in the air, he could see in his peripheral vision a large shadow moving in and hitting the fox like a battering ram.

When Joshua landed two seconds later he saw the wolf. Gray, large and holding the comparably small fox in his mouth. The wolf snarled and snapped the fox's neck in one bite. Joshua, still in absolute terror, thought of a way to escape the wolf and could only hope that the fox was enough food for him for a while. Then the wolf dropped the fox in front of him. They looked at each other for a moment.

"I have been tracking you for two days." The wolf's thoughts reached Joshua easily. "You should be more careful with your cover. From the air you must be an easy target with your red feathers against the grass."

Joshua, rather than prolonging this, thought he'd come right out with it.

"If you want to eat me, do it now. I'm tired, I need water and I can't escape you anyway. So, if you wouldn't mind, I'd rather get this over with."

Was the wolf smiling? Or was it the thought of a smile that reached Joshua. Either way, it was not at all what he had expected. It was rather unsettling.

"I'm not here to eat you."

The wolf sat down. Even now he was at least three times Joshua's height.

"I'm here to help you."

"Excuse me?" Joshua thought.

The wolf lay down.

"I am here to help you."

"Preposterous," Joshua thought.

"And yet, you are alive and well and a minute ago you were as good as dead."

Joshua could hardly escape the logic of the wolf's argument. "You might keep me alive until after you have eaten the fox," he thought, looking straight at the wolf.

"You make very little sense at the moment." The wolf replied. "But you are also probably still scared so I will not take it personally."

"Thank you." Joshua wasn't sure if he meant this ironically or if he just meant it. He was thankful, no doubt about that. A few moments ago, he was certain of his death. Now he was… safe? He couldn't remember when he had felt like this before. There were vague memories of a warm coop and the closeness of the chicks next to him when he was very young. But since he had been an adult… He realized at this moment that he didn't even know how very little he had felt safe. Until now. He sat across this scary looking, blue eyed, large wolf who could snap his neck without blinking an eye and he felt safe?

Despite the irrationality of this, there was a brief moment when Joshua decided to trust this feeling, to go with it, to embrace it. Trust. Put your life in someone else's hands. Trust… Just before he was about to lose the feeling again, giving way to fear once more, the wolf got up.

"There is a small creek, mostly underground, but I saw where it reaches the surface for a while. We should be able to make it there before nightfall."

And that was that. The wolf moved in front of him, leaving the grass slightly bent and much easier to navigate. Joshua followed. To where, he did not know. First he needed to get water and then see from there. One talon stride at a time.

* * *

"Grey."

"Excuse me?"

"My name is Grey, in case you were wondering."

Joshua was indeed just wondering what the wolf's name was. He still wasn't used to the instant communication between himself and the wolf. With the hens in his pen, talking to them was less immediate; the barrier between them thicker, as if there was a wall he first had to penetrate. With the wolf it seemed so clear.

At the wolf's suggestion, they were in the process of climbing a rather large hill. Mossy rocks and the long shadows of the dwarf pines gave it an eerie feel. The wolf didn't seem to notice. Nose on the ground he lead the way through the forest, sometimes stopping in his tracks, ears up and listening intently.

"Not far from here, on the other side, there is a small cave where we can stay during the night," he thought to Joshua as the image of a small cave appeared in his mind. It had begun to snow slightly and Joshua was glad when they reached the small cave. It was little more than an overhang in the rock, but it was large enough for both of them and there was a small tree growing under it. Joshua jumped up on one of the low branches.

"I will be right back," the wolf thought. "There is a nest of rabbits just below." And he was gone. Five minutes later he came back with two rabbits in his mouth. He entered the cave, lay down and started to eat them, clearly enjoying himself. Joshua watched from his branch, feeling a bit uneasy.

"I'll leave some for you, if you want," Grey's thoughts reached him.

"No. Thank you. I'm... fine."

"There were rabbits on the farm you lived in?"

"Yes. How do you know?"

"If you don't want everything around you to know what you are thinking, you will need to learn how to guard your thoughts better."

"I didn't know…"

"I can see what you are thinking, very clearly. And the answer is 'no'. I would not eat you, even if I were very hungry."

"I'm glad," Joshua replied, still uneasy about the subject. "There were about two dozen rabbits," he continued. "Every Sunday one was taken. Sometimes I wondered if I would be next. I didn't lay any eggs or have any other important functions to fulfill."

"You looked out for the hens and chicks. You kept them safe. That's a function."

Joshua's gaze grazed the moonlit valley below. His eyes stung suddenly. "I guess so. At least until I was silly enough to think I should go and leave and follow a dream. Since then there has been nothing but misery."

The wolf looked at him. His blue eyes seemed to penetrate deep into Joshua's soul. He couldn't look away. He could sense depth in the wolf and wisdom but behind that he saw sadness also. After a while an image came to him of a snow covered forest. There were icicles hanging from large pines, their branches almost touching the ground thick with snow. He saw a female wolf, her front paw in a trap. There was blood all around the large iron claw that had penetrated the wolf's skin and flesh deep into her bone. For three days Grey stayed with her, bringing her game for food. But when the hunters came on the fourth day they came to kill her. Grey fought them and killed one of them before he could raise his bow. The second hunter missed Grey by an inch but he was a great hunter from the villages by the wind gorges and his second arrow found the heart of his companion only moments after Grey had evaded the first. He wanted to die right then and there for his life seemed to have lost all its meaning without her on his side. He wanted to just step into the clearing and let the great hunter's arrow find his heart also. Maybe in death they could find each other again, he thought. But something in him wasn't ready for this yet. He just couldn't bring himself to do it. She wouldn't have wanted this, he realized. Like a warm wind from the highlands where the winds carry the warmth from the wide, sun-flooded valley up into the hills at night, it softly spoke to him of the life she wanted him to have.

So he stayed hidden until the night gave way to dawn and the hunter was gone and so was her body. He looked at the area where she had lain for three days but couldn't see any signs of her. The snow had covered everything. The blood and even her scent were gone. It was as if she had never existed.

The wolf ran for ten days crossing the Tundra, barely stopping, barely eating, and barely feeling anything. He had wished that he could just leave his loss and run away from it and never face it again. But it followed him like a hunter stalks his prey and on the eleventh day he slowed down and let his grief catch up with him. He sank to the ground and wept until he fell into a dreamless sleep. And when he woke the next morning the emptiness in his heart was as vast as the Tundra, and as cold.

"I'm sorry," Joshua thought. "I'm so sorry."

"Thank you," the wolf replied.

"You did all you could to help her."

"I know," Grey thought.

"You didn't leave her there. You stayed with her." Joshua was surprised about the bitterness that accompanied his thought.

"No. I didn't leave her. That doesn't make me feel less responsible. For it should have been me who died there in the cold, not her. I would have given everything for it to have been me. Everything and more."

There was no answer to that and Joshua felt the emptiness that enveloped the wolf at that moment and he realized that this emptiness was in his heart as well.

5. Krieg

O ver the next few days, Joshua and the wolf walked the land, crossing streams and climbing one hill only to walk down on the other side and up onto the next. Both stayed within their own thoughts for the most part until, on the third day, they were coming over yet another hill, when they saw an old barn amongst a small settlement of buildings.

"Do you feel this?" Joshua thought.

"No. What is it?" Grey answered.

"I have felt this before. In my pen. We were two roosters at first. But the other one was almost twice my size and he picked at me and the other hens constantly. One morning the door to the pen opened and the farmer came in and grabbed the other rooster and brought him to a spot next to the house. He laid him on a large block of wood and, at that moment, a wave of fear and terror reached me... from him... like nothing I have ever felt before."

"I felt the same from you just before I took the fox."

They looked at each other for a moment.

"There is something down there. It's a large animal and I think it's afraid of its life. We have to go help him!" Joshua replied. And without any further thought he flew down the hill and toward the large barn. Grey had no choice but to follow. "We should probably avoid settlements like this," he thought to Joshua.

"I know," Joshua answered. "We can't avoid this one."

Waves and waves of fear came from within the barn and Joshua had to muster every ounce of his strength not to be overcome by the strong feeling of terror.

He flew up to a window sill and peered inside. There were three men. Two of them held the rains of a huge horse. It must have been a war horse at some point. It was massive, dark brown with a black mane, white markings and extensive feathering. The third man held something that looked like a bolt gun. Joshua had seen this before on the farm. It had been used to slaughter pigs and cows. It was usually held to the animal's forehead and a bolt came out penetrating the scull and killing it instantly.

"They are going to kill him!" Joshua thought. "We have to do something!" He flew off the window sill and ran around the barn and through the open door. When he saw the horse from down here he was even bigger than before. He stood on his hind legs, fear clearly showing in his eyes. Joshua flew up in the air, screaming loudly while trying to lure the men's attention toward him. The one with the bolt gun tried to kick him several times and Joshua evaded him each time but barely.

"Let's get this over with!" One of the other two men said. "I don't have all day! Get my rifle." He gestured toward a shelf on one of the walls. The man with the bolt gun turned towards it.

At that moment, the wolf stepped quietly into the barn. Everything slowed down. Joshua could see the dust particles in the air around Grey's head who stood in a beam of sunlight coming in from a gap in the barn siding. The man with the bolt gun saw him first. He was so stunned that he completely froze. The two others saw the man stop in his tracks and, following his gaze, saw the wolf as well. With a low snarl he stood, teeth bared, the coat at his neck standing up.

"You will never reach that rifle," Grey thought to the man closest to him. Not that the man understood his thoughts but he realized at that moment that he had no chance of reaching the rifle and shooting the wolf in time. He backed away.

The horse pulled his head backwards and the reign slipped out of one of the man's hands. The other couldn't hold his either and the horse was suddenly free. He stood up on his hind legs causing one of the men to fall backwards, nearly missing a blow from one of the horse's hooves. The image of the horse on its hind legs and the wolf standing across from it in the beam of light inside the barn was so powerful and awe inspiring in Joshua's eyes that for one moment he forgot the terror he felt.

Then all hell broke loose as the wolf charged at the man with the nail gun. Joshua was struck by the men's screams and fear for their lives. It was equal to the horse's panic from just a minute ago. As the wolf hit the man and pushed him to the ground, the horse jumped over both of them and bolted through the open door. Joshua thought at first that the wolf would kill the man but then he realized that he was just standing on the man's chest, his bared teeth only inches away from the man's face. He was in absolute terror.

"We should go!" Joshua thought to the wolf. "GREY!" He yelled in his thoughts.

The wolf turned his head as if coming out of a trance. "We have to leave. Now!" For a moment longer the wolf looked at the man then he turned and ran outside, followed by Joshua.

They cleared the barn and Joshua saw Grey break through thick bushes and down an embankment to a small stream. "They are going to hunt us!" The wolf's thoughts reached Joshua as they made their way down the stream. Joshua flew most of the time but he knew he couldn't keep this up for much longer. "I'm too slow. I won't make it!" Joshua thought to the wolf. "If they catch me they'll catch you. You should run, Grey. They won't have any interest in a rooster if they can hunt a wolf."

"I will not leave you." The wolf thought.

"You will have to if you want to live."

Joshua felt his strength leaving him quickly. He wasn't used to flying or using his wings at all. In the last few days he had used them more than ever before in his life. Now he felt every push as a strain.

"Go!" He thought to the wolf. From a distance he could hear the men yelling to each other. He could only hear a few words. "Hunt. Kill. Wolf."

"I can take them!" The wolf replied.

"No you cannot. You cannot take three men with rifles. You must go!"

"I will not." And with that, Grey turned around and headed back toward the voices of the men.

"No, Grey!" Joshua yelled in his thoughts "You can't do this!"

At that moment, the horse broke through the underbrush just in front of the wolf. For a second horse and wolf looked at each other, a hint of fear in the horse's eyes. "Jump on my back," the horse thought to Joshua.

"What?"

"You heard right. Jump on my back and hold on to my mane. That's your only chance."

The wolf looked flustered. A rooster riding a horse?

"Do it. NOW! Or you just saved me for nothing."

Joshua made a conscious choice at that moment not to think about what would happen but rather to just do it. Without another thought he jumped, flew and landed on the horse's back.

"Hold on!" The horse thought and, with that, turned around and broke through the brush and into the open meadow. What followed was the wildest ride of Joshua's life. He dug his talons into the horse's back and if it felt it, it didn't let him know. He realized very quickly that he needed to stay low if he wanted to stay on at all.

The large warhorse flew across the meadow with the wolf at its side. Joshua felt the sheer power of the horse's muscles under him but he also felt its utter joy of having escaped certain death; of running fast as the wind, pushing against the earth beneath its hooves. Joshua couldn't help but be infected by this array of emotions and to his complete surprise he let out a rooster call that was filled with his own joy joined with the horse's. The call was heard in the farthest reaches of the valley by creatures large and small and some of them felt the joy inside their hearts as well. And for the smallest of moments they were all with him.

* * *

They eventually slowed down into a trot and by nightfall they rested by a small stream that flowed into a still pond. The cover of snow that had fallen earlier made the night even quieter. Joshua sat on a low branch in a large pine tree. Grey lay below him on the pine needles licking his paws. They were raw from the day of running on the harsh ground. The horse stood by the edge of the pond grazing off a small patch that was more dirt than grass. His reins were tangled with small branches and covered in mud from the escape. Joshua could feel the throbbing pain the horse had in his mouth from the metal reins pulling at it all day.

"I can take these off for you if you want," the wolf thought. Joshua saw in his mind's eye the image of the horse lying down in front of the wolf and Grey, with his teeth, taking the leather strips of the reins and pulling them over the horse's head.

The war horse turned his head and looked at Grey for a moment. There was hesitation in his eyes. It was accompanied by another image the three of them shared. It was of such brutality that the wolf got up suddenly, his neck hair standing up and his upper lip pulling back, teeth bared. Joshua let out a terrified rooster call and flew down from his branch. It was a scene from a war. There were dead soldiers everywhere and blood mixed with the dark soil in the ground. A group of eight horses huddled together near a barren tree on the vast battlefield. The tree was their only shelter. They had mud and dried blood all over them. Some of the blood was their own; some came from the soldiers who fought on them or whom they fought against. There were dead horses among the men; their bodies seemed peaceful as if they had escaped the terror of the battle at last. The few soldiers that were left took care of the wounded.

There was suddenly movement on the edge of the field. Something drew near. Through the fog it was hard to make out at first. But then the horses caught the scent and terror spread among them like wildfire. The pack of wolves that came out of the high grass looked like an image straight from the depths of hell. They were starved and starving, filthy, eyes red with blood lust standing clearly in them. Without warning they leaped forward toward the horses. The horses, worn and tired beyond comprehension from days of battle did not have the strength to flee. The wolves moved quickly and Joshua saw their horse. He stood on the edge of the group watching as one of the wolves flew toward him, jumping, mouth open wide with claws ready to rip into his flesh. The only thing the horse could do at this moment was move forward and meet the wolf in mid air. The horse stood up on his hind legs and jumped. He and the wolf met and for a moment, were face to face.

The image of the wolf's face so close to his own was burned into the horse's mind and even though now safe and far away from the battlefield, it took all possible control for him not to take off and run— run away from it and never confront it again.

"How did you escape?" Joshua asked after a while.

"I don't remember," the horse answered. "All I know is that I never saw the others again. I don't know if they survived or what became of them."

"I'm sorry," the wolf thought into the silence. Then he walked over to the horse and lay down in front of it. His head on his paws he looked up at the large war horse.

"I can help you with your reins," he quietly thought to him.

As the horse looked at the wolf, the moon broke through the clouds illuminating the snow covered ground and reflecting in the still pond. For a while the horse stood motionless. Then it went down on its front legs and lay on the ground across from the wolf. Joshua watched from a short distance as Grey slowly got up and walked toward the horse. Without hesitation he took the bridle in his mouth right between the horse's ears and slowly pulled on the leather strip. It slid off and the horse was free.

"Thank you," the horse thought.

"No," the wolf replied. "I thank you."

"What is your name?" Joshua asked after a moment

"Krieg," the war horse answered.

"What does it mean, Krieg?"

"It means 'war'. Just 'war'. I was bred for the war, born during the war and trained for battle.

"Is that where all your scars come from?" Joshua asked.

The horse looked toward the dark horizon, lost in his thoughts.

"I have seen death and too much of it. On the battlefields of Toloose where men fought men for land that belonged to neither. For riches that held no value other than a handful of sand that amounted to nothing. I saw blood there that ran like crimson rivers across the charred soil. It spilled from brothers and fathers and sons, from big hearts and small ones and the blood of each flowed into the others' and in death they became one once again and they forgot why it was they had fought."

He turned toward Joshua and the Wolf. "I just want peace. I do not wish to fight for my life anymore. I'm too old. Too tired. Soon. Soon, I will follow my fathers' path into the great vast grasslands where the sun never sets and the water is plenty, and where there is peace for all living things. Until then, I am in your debt, Joshua. In both of yours. Until then, tell me how—"

"You are not indebted to me, Krieg. Not in the slightest," Joshua answered. "Anyone would have done the same for you."

"Be that as it may, red one, the debt stands until it is paid. To both of you. End of discussion."

All was still after Krieg spoke. Joshua looked from the horse to the wolf, letting his eyes rest on each of them for a moment. He realized that the two creatures would probably not be friends under normal circumstances. But under normal circumstances neither of the three would likely be friends with either of the other two.

"I had a dream." Joshua thought into the silence. "A dream of three feathers somewhere in the depths below the Storm Mountains. In my dream the feathers were so dear to me and I to them that I want to find them. I am not sure what they mean or if they mean anything at all, but I know in my heart that I must find them, even though I do not know why." As he looked at the others, he knew that they saw what he saw—an immense cave with the three feathers resting on a black, polished cylinder of stone.

"I will help you," Krieg thought. "Your peace is mine, Joshua of the Great Lake."

"And mine," Grey added.

The night held its breath for a moment. The moon stood low and clear in the sky and it seemed as if everything around them became a quiet witness to this pact. And Joshua, for the smallest of instants, had an inkling of what it means to have companions by his side.

6. **W**ater

They walked for three days, crossing a valley that stretched out for miles before them, and passing through a densely wooded forest where the branches built a thick roof above their heads. They rested by small streams where they stilled their thirst. Grey caught a few large fish and there was more than plenty of food for Krieg and Joshua. And all the while, they shared with each other their stories and their lives as they remembered them. They shared their fears and joys, their shortcomings and their triumphs. But most of all they came to know what each of them longed for. Krieg's deep wish for peace, Grey's longing for the love of his dead companion and Joshua's powerful dream that he felt he could no longer live without. On the end of the fourth day they knew of each other what seldom is known except in long and deep friendships.

As they walked, the weather changed. They left behind the snowy hills and reached an area where the sun lay on fields of grass that was just about to spring up through the frozen soil. Soon the first blossoms would be visible, pushing through the darkness towards the sunlight. The three friends felt that the spring around them that was about to meet the last days of winter, mirrored their own journey, their own leaving behind their past and venturing toward something bigger, still unknown but no longer completely hidden from them. Then the howling began.

They had just settled down for the night when they heard it. First it came from one direction. Then another and yet another.

"Wolves?" Was Joshua's first thought.

"No," Krieg answered. "Those wolves I encountered a long time ago were bred for the war, starved by their masters to feed on the fear of the survivors. I have not encountered them since.

"Krieg is right," Grey thought. "Those aren't wolves. I would know. What I do know is that whatever it is, it has by now completely surrounded us.

"What shall we do?" Joshua asked.

"Jump on my back," the horse thought to Joshua.

Before Joshua could follow Krieg's thought, he saw an image of a pack of Hyenas in his mind coming from the wolf.

"A dozen of them. Maybe two. I can take four, maybe five, but a dozen? I have no chance against them. We have to run."

"Jump!" The horse thought to Joshua. As Joshua jumped, wings fluttering, onto the warhorses back, the wolf charged in the opposite direction.

"I'll divert them," he thought. "I can outrun them easily." And he was gone—a gray shadow disappearing into the dark of night.

Three of the hyenas appeared and charged toward Joshua and Krieg who went on his hind legs and jumped forward. The hyenas changed direction to cut off their escape path. As they came closer, Joshua saw their large fangs and powerful jaws snapping at the horse's legs.

"Hold on tight!" Krieg's thought reached him just at the moment when the horse changed direction as well and went straight into the path of the two hyenas to his right. He trampled them, his powerful hooves crushing them and pushing them into the ground. The third one evaded the hooves, but barely. It held its distance knowing that the rest of the pack would catch up soon.

"Can you outrun them?" Joshua asked Krieg.

"I don't know but we'll find out very soon," he thought.

The howling now came from ahead of them as well. The eerie cries of the hyenas made Joshua's skin crawl.

"Don't be afraid," Krieg thought to him. "They will feed on your fear and that fear will come back to you twice as strong. It will make you weak."

"I can't help it," Joshua thought. "There seem to be so many!"

As they galloped through the night, yellow eyes watching them from all directions and the cries from the hyenas coming ever closer, it dawned on Joshua that they might not make it.

"Follow me!" Grey was suddenly next to them. He turned to the right. Krieg changed direction and followed the wolf's lead.

Through the pounding of the hooves and the eerie cries of the hyenas, Joshua suddenly heard something else. Something loud and powerful. It came closer fast.

"What is that?" He thought.

"Water!" Joshua caught the glimpse of an image from Krieg.

"Water?" The thought hung in front of Joshua for a moment and through the sheer blackness of the night Joshua suddenly saw a river next to them. It was flowing fast, almost as fast as they ran.

The hyenas closed in on them from the other side. The three companions were trapped between the pack of hyenas and the raging river.

"But why is it so loud all of the sudden?" Joshua was overwhelmed by the deafening sound of the water. The answer hit him an instant later.

"It's a waterfall. We have to stop! We are going directly toward a waterfall!" Joshua cried out. In his panic he dug his talons deeper into the skin of the horse.

"We can't stop. Not anymore. HOLD ON!" The horse's thoughts hit Joshua. He felt Krieg's and Grey's utter desperation, joined with his own.

Krieg pushed through the last of the high grass bushes and was suddenly suspended in mid air. Joshua let go of the horse's back, lifting off, his wings unfolding. He saw Grey jump as well. Joshua felt gravity pulling him down. He struggled to land on a small tree-like branch jutting out of the rock. From there he watched Krieg and Grey fall and crash into the icy water fifteen feet below.

Then he saw two of the Hyenas fall over the edge. They couldn't stop in time and fell down as well. Krieg and the wolf tried to swim to the side of the large pool but the current was too strong. They were inevitably pulled into a second waterfall and moments later disappeared over the edge. Joshua thought about it only for a second before he spread his wings again and flew down. He couldn't swim so hitting the water was not an option.

When he was above the second waterfall he realized that this one was much higher than the first. At least fifty feet. The noise was deafening. Joshua barely made it over the edge without crashing into the water, nearly missing one of the hyenas. He looked into its eyes and felt his own fear reflected in them. Then it went over the edge.

The mist of the falls clung to his feathers making them heavier as he tried very hard not to lose too much height. There was a rock sticking out of the water far down from where he was. He had to make it there and land on it, otherwise he would certainly drown. He saw Grey and Krieg swimming toward it and hoped they would reach it as well.

He realized that if he stretched his wings just a tiny bit outward he wouldn't have to struggle so much to stay in the air. "Who says roosters can't fly!" He thought when suddenly a gust of wind pushed him down and toward the water. He was completely unprepared and could only counter it with one or two flaps of his wings before he crashed into the water. He went under, immediately pushed down by a strong undercurrent. Instinctively he held his breath but it became clear to him that he had only a few seconds before he would pass out.

"Where are you?" He heard Grey in his thoughts.

"Under water," was the only thing he could think of in his panic.

For a moment nothing seemed to happen. Joshua was picked up by another undercurrent and pushed to the side, upside down turning over and over under water.

"Hold on to me!" He heard Grey.

Joshua, more out of instinct than anything else, dug his talons into what he thought was the fur of the wolf's hind leg.

"Don't let go!" Grey swam toward the surface and was almost there when another strong current took hold of Joshua and he lost his grip. Luckily this brought him to the surface where he flapped weakly while trying desperately to get air into his lungs.

Suddenly he was grabbed by sharp teeth. For a moment he thought it was one of the hyenas but then the teeth very gently pulled him out of the water without so much as a scratch. Grey carried Joshua onto the small island and dropped him on the stone. One of the hyenas tried to climb onto the island as well but Krieg just stood there looking at it. The hyena let go eventually and was, seconds later, swept away by the current.

The wolf shook himself, water spraying in all directions. Joshua, unable to move, was exhausted beyond anything he had experienced before in his life. He couldn't lift even a wing.

"Are you hurt?" The horse asked.

"I don't think so."

"You should try to shake out your feathers. Otherwise they might freeze during the night."

"It's not over yet," Grey's thoughts reached both.

"What do you mean?" Joshua replied.

"We have to swim across to the shore. This is just an island and we can't stay here for long."

"We should wait until morning and then swim over," Krieg replied.

"I don't think that's a good idea," Grey answered. "This island is very low and close to the water. If it starts to rain, it might flood. If the river swells, the current will be even stronger."

Joshua lifted his head and shook it. "I don't think I can make it. Can't we just stay?"

"I can take you on my back. I agree with the wolf. We can't stay here."

"There is something else." The wolf's gaze went beyond the edge of the water.

"What?" Joshua tried to stand up but sat back down immediately, a wave of dizziness going through him.

"Hollow's Gate."

"Hollow's Gate?" Joshua asked.

"It was called The Big Deep in ancient times," Krieg answered. "Many wars have been fought over it and because of it. It is said it holds riches that nobody can comprehend. No one ever came back from it except the eagles and only because they were able to use the upward winds to return."

"What is it?" Joshua asked. He had heard of it from birds and geese that either lived at the farm or had taken rest in one of the small pools of water on their way north. What he had heard were only legends. According to them it was a place clouded in darkness and only creatures who avoided the light lived there. Hollow's Gate was a gorge, fifty miles in diameter, swallowing everything that came near it, even the air to breathe.

"The walls that surround it," Grey thought, "are straight. A sheer cliff dropping at least five thousand feet down. There is no path to the bottom that I know of and there certainly is no way back up. We have to bypass it completely if we were to get to Storm Mountain."

"The current here is very strong," Joshua thought. He could see the water moving rapidly toward the edge and from there into nothingness.

"If we fall over the edge we will die." Grey's matter-of-factness was strangely comforting.

As if on cue, it started to rain. Joshua was tired beyond belief. The cold made him shiver and the thought of having to cross the rushing water was almost paralyzing.

"Let's do it," he thought to the others. "Krieg, if I fall off your back, I want you both to try to make it to other side. Do not worry about me." He tried to sound much stronger than he was and much more forceful. Grey and Krieg just looked at each other as if to say, "Sure, we'll leave you to go to your certain death while we save ourselves. It is just not going to happen."

Joshua got up, tried to shake out as much water as he could. His wings felt as if they were dipped in lead. He could barely walk but when the horse went down to his front legs and lay down, he climbed up onto its massive back.

"We will make it," Krieg thought to him.

"I hope you are right," Joshua thought back. He wasn't convinced.

"That you don't trust your own strength doesn't mean I don't have any left. It also doesn't mean you can't trust mine," the horse thought.

"There is no arguing with that," Josh thought to himself more than to the others.

The horse stood up and walked to the edge of the small island. The wolf stood next to them. It was at least a hundred feet to the other side and there wasn't much room for error. The thought of death wasn't even the most disconcerting in Joshua's mind. What terrified him more than anything was the thought of just disappearing into a fathomless gorge that would swallow them into oblivion.

Before he could dwell any further, Krieg went into the water and was immediately caught by the current. Grey, upstream from them, went in as well. The current was much stronger than they expected.

What followed now was one of the most terrifying ordeals in Joshua's life. One of the reasons for it was that he had no control at all, not of the current and not of Krieg's movement through the rushing water. Several times he was submerged and could barely hold on to Krieg's mane. Too slowly, they made their way across. The edge seemed to come closer much faster than the other side. Grey was pushed against Krieg who was heavier and floated slightly slower than the wolf. At one point Joshua thought that the horse would topple over but he somehow managed to stay upright.

Hot panic suddenly rose inside him when he realized that they wouldn't make it across in time. There was too much distance left. He had visions of them falling over the edge and disappearing into utter blackness. He also realized that his weight, albeit not that much, caused additional strain to Krieg who was struggling as it was to not be swept away by the strong current.

"I don't think we'll make it!" Joshua thought. "I'm going to try to fly over!"

"No!" Krieg's thoughts left no room for doubt or opposition in Joshua's mind. "Stay where you are." As they moved toward the edge, too fast and with utter inevitability, Joshua suddenly found himself back in the coop, huddled up against the other chickens to keep warm, not quite awake but also not completely asleep. There was comfort there and warmth. Part of him wanted to just go back there in his mind and stay there, hold on to it until the fall over the edge would kill him eventually. It wouldn't be that painful, he thought. Just slip away. Let go of this tortured body and—"

"Joshua!" The wolf stood in his mind, teeth bared. Joshua's thoughts were pulled back from the edge. He felt the horse's panic under his talons. He saw Grey fighting for his life. The thought that he could not do anything to help them overwhelmed him and pushed away the fear for his own life.

"No!" He thought. "There must be something I can do." And with that he jumped up in the air, lifted off the back of the horse and flew toward the other side. He knew he probably wouldn't make it but he thought that without his weight on Krieg's back, the horse might have a fighting chance to reach safety. He gained about ten feet of height and for a moment he caught a glimpse over the edge. But there was only blackness. Once he flew up, his strength left him almost immediately and it was as if his tortured muscles just stopped responding to his command to fly. He dropped and hit the water, the current instantly taking him and pushing him toward the edge. Krieg and Grey no longer tried to get to shore but swam toward him. Suddenly, while his body was turned over and over by the current and losing all sense of where he was, he remembered that he saw a small path to the side of the falls as if carved into the stone. Large enough to carry a horse.

"When you go over the edge try to jump to the right. There is a path!" He yelled in his thoughts, not knowing if the others would even hear him. Then he felt sharp rock under his talons and a push from the side. With that, he was catapulted into the night and out of the water. For a moment he thought he fell into nothingness but an instant later he landed on rock, tumbled a few feet and lay still. He drifted in and out of consciousness and went from blackness to blurry images of the wolf and the horse standing over him, cascades of water dripping down from them.

"We are safe," he heard Grey in his thoughts. And when he heard it he knew it was true and he fell into a deep sleep and he dreamed of a large cave and three feathers on a blackened stone and of three companions and the bond they shared.

* * *

When he awoke the next morning, the sun was high in the sky and Joshua found himself huddled against the wolf's belly. His whole body hurt when he tried to move his wings. Krieg stood a few feet away trying to find grass on the rocky ground. The whole side of the horse was covered in abrasions.

"Are you hurt?" He asked him.

"I'll live. Nothing life threatening. I'm glad to have those. Scraping over the stones was what slowed me down enough to make the jump."

"How did we...? I can't remember anything." Joshua's vision was still blurry as he tried to find his balance on the rocky ground.

"We made it just in time," Grey thought to both of them. "I'm glad you live. For a while we weren't sure if you would make it."

There was no reason to relive something that Joshua couldn't remember so he didn't pursue it any further. As he began to walk around the wolf he saw that Grey had blood on his coat as well.

"We're pretty beat up," he thought.

The wolf smiled in his thoughts. "That we are."

"Aren't you glad you saved me from the fox?" Not waiting for an answer he stepped around and now got a full view of where they were.

To their left the waterfall disappeared into the abyss below. To their right there was a path cut into the stone, into the sheer cliff. The path lead away from the plateau they stood on. How far it went Joshua could not see, but it seemed as if it went slightly downward. This could have been an optical illusion, for the massive wall of rock that disappeared into the fog below, curved in the distance and it looked as if, tens of miles in diameter, the wall of stone made a large circle ending on the other side of the waterfall next to them.

"What now?" Joshua asked. "We can't go back. We can't go down there."

"There is only one way for us to go and it is to follow along the path in front of us." Grey got up. "There is no path for us to take but this one."

As it had happened before, Joshua could not escape the logic in the wolf's thoughts.

"We leave in the morning," Krieg thought to them. "Find some rest. We might need it."

The remainder of the day Joshua spent sleeping and once in a while looking for food on the rocky ground. The sound of the waterfall was their constant companion. It was at times calming and at others unsettling. Each time he drifted into sleep he dreamed of falling endlessly until he awoke, shaking from the cold and the terror of it. He asked Krieg twice if they could just go now instead of waiting here. There was no food for the wolf and he was worried that there wouldn't be any for a while. Joshua could always find something on the ground and Krieg would probably always find grass somewhere but the wolf couldn't survive without eating for more than a couple of days.

"I will be fine," Grey answered his thoughts. "Do not be concerned about me."

As they looked at each other Joshua realized for the first time how completely different they were. They had, under normal circumstances, absolutely nothing in common except perhaps the one thing that one was hunter the other prey. And yet, here they were, at the edge of an abyss with nothing but each other to rely on.

"Why did you help me?" He asked into the silence.

"What do you mean?" Grey answered.

"When I stood before the fox hole, why did you help me?"

For a long while the wolf did not respond. All Joshua saw in his mind were fleeting images of Grey's companion when both roamed the ice forests together.

"I do not know the answer." The wolf looked at him. "I just knew I had to. The... longing in you was so strong and powerful I wanted to help you find whatever it was you are looking for. Maybe so I could find whatever it is I'm searching for as well."

"So far we have been pretty successful, don't you think?" Joshua wasn't quite sure if he meant this as a joke.

"It could be worse," the wolf answered.

They both smiled in their thoughts. And when night came and then dawn and the morning painted the sky in colors of deepest orange, they were ready to continue on their journey.

7. Wind

oshua sat on Krieg's back as they made their way along the slightly descending path. The smooth granite-like rock to their right went straight up and the further they went the larger became the distance between them and the top of the cliff. Joshua imagined a large spiral going downward ever deeper into an unknown world that he didn't really want to enter. What if they would have to keep walking indefinitely? It could take weeks for them to travel the distance circling ever deeper and not knowing what awaited them at the bottom.

The further they went, the more he began to feel Krieg's restlessness. As if the horse had to actively stop himself from falling into a trot. When Joshua looked back at one point, he saw the waterfall far in the distance at the end of a slightly curving path. All of it still lay in the shadows. The sun was still low on the horizon and it did not yet reach them from the other side of the valley.

As they made their way along the path, Joshua couldn't help wonder why he went on this journey to begin with. Doubts rose in his mind—doubts of the justification of all this. Was it all worth it? He began to think that whatever it was that had pushed or pulled him to go and leave his world, his place of belonging, was probably just a dream, no more than the senseless musings of a bored existence. Why, in all the world, did he have to go and fly out of the pen? Nothing seemed more preposterous at that moment and he felt himself slipping into a deep hopelessness grounded in the utter lack of purpose the journey suddenly seemed to have.

"There is something ahead of us," Krieg's thoughts brought him back. At that moment Joshua realized that the thoughts he had, the feelings of hopelessness that had occupied his mind were not solely his. The origin of it however was unclear, clouded in mist and veiled from him. A heart-rending howl escaped the wolf suddenly and Krieg jumped forward and fell into a gallop. Joshua thought he saw something further down the path sticking out of the smooth rock. Looking into the fog far below them and having the sheer cliff going upward to his right, Joshua was afraid that they would inevitably lose their footing and fall down if they were to continue to gallop like this. He forced himself to concentrate on holding on to Krieg's coat and mane.

"What do you think it is?" He asked, mostly to distract himself from thinking about the sheer drop to his left and the claustrophobic closeness of the rock to his right.

"I don't know," Krieg answered."

"I'm not so sure about this," the wolf thought from behind them. "We should be careful."

Suddenly, out of nowhere, a path split off from the one they traveled on and lead upward toward the top of the cliffs in a steep incline. It looked like a small, washed out and dry narrow creek bed. They stopped.

"This most likely leads up to the top of the cliff," Grey thought. "I suggest we follow it."

"From there we could just walk along the edge and bypass this altogether," Joshua thought. Krieg moved restlessly. Joshua felt that the horse wanted to stay on their path until they found whatever it was that was further down.

"It's up to you, Joshua," Krieg thought. "We can go up here. It's steep but we'll make it."

Joshua felt the horse's conflict and made up his mind before Krieg could form another thought.

"Let's go further down and find out what it is that sleeps there. Afterwards we'll come back and go up the path to the top."

He felt the horse's agreement and they silently continued down the path.

"Do you see this? There is something in the rock there," Grey thought.

"I see it too. It seems to stick out of the side of the cliff," Joshua answered.

"Wait." Krieg stopped.

"What is it?" Joshua asked.

"Let me go alone," Krieg thought.

"Why?" Grey asked.

"I don't know, but whatever it is that lays there, it might not be the best way to be woken up by a wolf standing over it."

"You have a point. But what if it's dangerous?" Grey thought.

"Then I'll come back up and we'll go the other way," the horse replied.

Joshua could see a small plateau in the shadows where the unrecognizable shape was sticking out of the cliffs. He flew off the horses back.

"Be careful," he thought.

"I will be," Krieg answered. "Keep your distance. If we have to run, I don't want you too close to whatever this is."

With that, the horse began to trot down the path. When he was about a hundred feet away, Joshua and Grey followed slowly. Krieg reached the plateau and stopped before a sculpture of stone that seemed to be half melted into the cliff. At that moment, the sun came over the rim of Hollow's Gate, illuminating the spot where Krieg stood. And now, out of the shadow and completely in the light, Joshua and Grey saw what it was. The head was slightly smaller than Krieg's, its features softer, more feminine. Its front hooves stood up from the ground and its back was melted into the stone cliff. With massive wings on either side, the stone Pegasus looked as if it were about to take flight.

The sun illuminated its ivory colored surface. As Joshua and Grey came closer, they saw the Pegasus' expression. Its eyes were closed in contentment as if she had willingly sought out this spot and also her state of being. Joshua had heard of the legends of the flying horses that lived in a city deep down in Hollow's Gate. But that was a long, long time ago. So long ago, it was almost forgotten.

Krieg's head was only inches away from the head of the stone Pegasus. It was as if he dared not breathe out of fear to disturb the creature. Joshua and Grey now stood on either side of the horse. Joshua felt… he wasn't quite sure, but he could only describe it as awe. The magnificent beauty of the creature was unlike anything he had ever seen before. And yet there was a sense of finality he felt while looking at her face. It crept up inside him and into his chest and made him gasp for air. Suddenly, Krieg stepped backwards and went on his hind legs letting out a cry that seemed to come out of sheer desperation. The wolf and Joshua moved backwards away from him. The horse started to pace back and forth, going on his hind legs several times and crying out each time.

"What is it, Krieg?" Joshua thought to him.

There was no answer from the horse just a sense of desperation sweeping over Joshua that he had to shake himself to get rid of.

"Krieg, what's going on?" He thought, hoping to get through to the horse.

Then the wolf began to wince and howl, as if in utter pain. It was the most eerie thing Joshua had ever heard. That, mixed with the horse's cries, made the scene turn into something completely otherworldly. It seemed as if the wolf, the horse and the stone Pegasus shared in something that Joshua was not part of, or only on the periphery.

"Grey. GREY!" He yelled in his thoughts. There was no answer. The wolf looked at him unable to communicate. Krieg began to frantically kick the stone around the Pegasus' hind legs but to no avail.

Finally, he stopped. So did Grey's howling. "I can't save her," Krieg thought to them. "She wanted to be here. It was her choice to be frozen in stone for all eternity for what she did. But once it happened she realized that it was a mistake, that she shouldn't be in here. And now she can't escape. She hasn't been able to escape for more than 900 years."

Joshua could feel Krieg's sense of helplessness. All the strength, endurance, and power of this mighty war horse were no match for the stone.

"Is there something we can do?" Joshua asked.

"No." Krieg answered.

When he looked at Joshua, his eyes spoke to him more than anything.

"I have fought many wars. I have seen despair in friend and foe. I have seen pain and loss and plenty of it but nothing captures my heart more than someone's inability to fight for freedom."

Grey and Joshua looked at each other, sharing in their friend's sorrow. Krieg walked close to the Pegasus and laid his head on the stone. Joshua watched as a single tear dropped down from the eyes of the war horse and landed on the head of the Pegasus.

All was quiet. Suddenly it was as if the air became denser around the plateau on which they stood. Something moved even though nothing was visible to the naked eye. There was a stirring and each of them felt it deep within themselves as if something inside each of them, something that was captured and held prisoner a long time ago, was finally set free. Joshua and the wolf stepped back. Was it a trick their mind played on them, an optical illusion of sorts, when some of the stone feathers of the Pegasus' massive wings began to move slightly in the wind?

Joshua realized at that moment that they were witnessing something that had not happened in eons, if ever. At that moment he became aware of the Pegasus. Not her features, but her mind. It was as if it had been submerged deep within her and finally found its way to the surface. There was an utter lightness to her being. Her mind was like a fountain of clear water sparkling in the sun. The sense of relief in her was so contagious that Joshua closed his eyes and let it envelop him completely.

When he opened his eyes, he saw her wings begin to move. The sheer joy of her slowly regaining freedom had no boundaries. The wind streaming off her massive wings pushed Joshua down to the ground and suddenly there was a rumbling from deep inside the mountain, as if it finally released her into freedom. The sound of the compressed air below her wings was like thunder. And then they heard a crack. Like a lightning strike, it went through them. Joshua didn't know what was happening at first. It all seemed to occur in slow motion. He saw the Pegasus on her hind legs, her massive wings moving up and down. He saw Krieg standing to the side watching. Joshua felt more than saw the wolf, slightly behind him across from the Pegasus and toward the edge of the Plateau.

Suddenly the ground beneath them gave way. At first Joshua thought that Krieg and the Pegasus, together with the cliff behind them, moved away from him. But then he realized that he and Grey were moving away from them. At that moment he knew what the cracking sound was. A large part of the plateau on which they stood was breaking off, taking him and the wolf with it and disappearing into the depth below. And then he fell.

8. Jump

rieg saw Joshua and the wolf disappear over the cliff. It took all his strength not to jump after them, but he knew that this would be certain death. The Pegasus was still partially embedded in the stone when Krieg saw that the path began to crumble and break off.

"We have to leave!" He thought to the Pegasus. "We have to leave now!"

The Pegasus looked around in panic trying frantically to free herself. "Help me!" The thought stood clearly in Krieg's mind. "I don't want to die and I'm still too weak to fly."

He began to kick the rock next to her with his hind legs. The stone began to loosen but not fast enough for him. The path back to safety crumbled more and more but suddenly the Pegasus was free.

"Run!" She thought to him.

She didn't have to tell him twice. He took off racing up the crumbling path. The moment they stepped off the plateau, it broke off and disappeared into the depth below. It was now as if the destruction of the path raced Krieg and the Pegasus. As fast as they ran, the breaking of the path gained on them until the Pegasus' hind legs were already pushing off loose rock.

"Here it is!"

Krieg jumped up and into the steep incline of the creek bed. The Pegasus followed and they both ran up the slippery path.

"Don't stop. Just keep going!" He reassured her.

As they made their way up the steep mountain side, the entire path up to the waterfall began to crumble and break off. And when Krieg and the Pegasus finally reached the top, there was nothing left of the path below. The sheer cliff was smooth, without any interruption as if the path and the plateau had never existed.

Panting, they stood on top of the cliff. Krieg's joy of having escaped certain death was overshadowed by the pain of losing his friends. He still couldn't believe what happened. Krieg had lost many fellow war horses and each one was as painful as the last. The sense of loss was a familiar one to him.

"I'm so sorry." The Pegasus must have heard his thoughts. When he looked at her, he saw it in her eyes—the knowledge of her having gained her life at the price of someone else losing theirs. She suddenly lost her balance and sank to the ground. Krieg stepped toward her not quite sure what to do.

"I wished for someone to come and free me for so long. I knew I couldn't do it on my own. And then I felt your footsteps on the path and there was the small hope that maybe this time... Several travelers came before you, but I never felt an anger so strong or the will to live and to give life that I felt in you. When you stopped at the fork I hoped you would come and try."

"I think I heard you." Krieg thought.

"I didn't know that death would be the price for my freedom," the Pegasus replied.

"Many of my fellow war horses died for me in the war, as I would have died for them. But we live and we must honor those who died not with more death but with our lives. Otherwise they died in vain."

As the sun rose behind them, flooding the landscape with golden light, Krieg could feel that, despite his words of wisdom he knew to be true, the loss of his friends cut deeper than he wanted to admit. There might be another battle for him to fight—the battle between the promise of a good life as payment to them and the sheer finality of losing their companionship. Only time would tell.

* * *

The next day passed in a haze for Krieg. They found a spring a little further south that carried clear cold water through a meadow where the snow and ice had melted almost completely.

"It will take me some time to get my strength back," the Pegasus thought to Krieg. "And when it comes back I will go and look for your friends. For I know your thoughts are burdened with their absence. But do not trust a hope. Time flows at a different speed at the bottom of Hollow's Gate than it does up here. You can spend one day at the surface and it will be close to a week below. 'The Great Deep', as it was called, has its own laws and what you believe now might not be true down there."

"You are saying that Grey and the red one have been down there for almost a week now?" Krieg could not fathom that they lay dead somewhere at the bottom of an ancient world where their bodies had already began to disintegrate.

"Do not let your thoughts go there," the Pegasus interrupted his thoughts. "It is a dark place from which you cannot see."

Krieg looked at her. He could sense her lightness of being below his grief. This lightness was something he had not yet found within himself. "You never told me your name."

"My name is Wind," she replied. "I got it when I first learned to fly."

"I always thought the legends spoke of Pegasus foals that could fly right out of the womb," Krieg answered.

There was a pause when she looked at him.

"No one has told you."

"No one has told me what?" Krieg replied.

"No one has told you how a Pegasus gets her wings?"

Krieg saw a smile in her that suddenly seemed to flood through him as well.

"You are telling me that you never knew how we get our wings?"

"No."

"That is so sad, Krieg. You must know that I was not born with wings. None of us is."

"What do you mean?"

"I mean having wings is not something we are given with birth even though it is our birth right. Don't you know that we are horses?"

"Horses?" Krieg was puzzled.

"Yes, horses. Krieg, we are horses that learned to go past our limitations. We have been given the chance to fly, to leave behind all that limits us and soar with the eagles high above the earth. We have been given freedom, Krieg."

For a while he was quiet. He became aware of the land around him and her presence next to him.

"How do you leave your limitations behind?" He asked.

Wind looked at him for a long time. There was a kindness in her eyes born of knowing the strength it took, the faith in both the goal and the means to reach it.

"Your limitations, you must not believe them. You must not fuel them with doubt about yourself. You must know they are not and have never been part of you. You must know yourself. And not only must you know yourself you must love it as well. Deep within, you must love… you."

Krieg was quiet for a while. Within himself there was a small part, deeply submerged somewhere, that resonated with her thoughts. At that moment he knew that her words were true. But…

"…you are asking, what about the other part? The part that thinks you small and frail and puny?" Wind finished his thought.

"Yes."

"You freed me from eternal imprisonment. I will help you go beyond your limits. I will help you get your wings. I will see you fly."

The last part of her thought whispered to him. Krieg's eyes stung suddenly and he closed them to hide what he felt. It was as if his whole life, all his struggles, the preparation for war, war itself and all the horrors it brought, the time when he was captured and held prisoner, his friends freeing him and his pain of losing them again, flowed like small streams joining together towards a great river. He suddenly knew that his life was culminating in this. Not only that, but each step along the way had been a step toward it. He just never knew that that was the goal all along. Why did he never even have the slightest inclination that he could one day leave all that he thought would limit him behind? Or could he?

He suddenly felt tired. "I'm not so sure I can make it. I'm old and the strength it takes to undertake this might be for younger steeds, more spirited horses, not an old war horse like myself."

And with that he closed the door that Wind had opened. The sting of regret was easier to handle than the thought to even question his limits. It would never happen. And that was the end of it.

* * *

It began just before dawn the next day. Krieg had just awoken from a deep sleep. He caught the faintest sense of joy when he awoke. It fled from him when he opened his eyes. The sky was clear above him. Wind slept next to him, her ivory coat had a slight glow from the light of the half moon that stood low on the horizon. Suddenly the Pegasus woke. She jumped to her feet as if shaking off a dream.

"The beacon!" She thought urgently. "Come!"

She ran. Krieg had no choice other than to follow her. Her graceful strides, wings half unfolded, captured him and, for a moment, the wish to be like her overcame him. The wish to be free fueled him and let him gain on her until they were side by side, racing through the moonlit meadow and toward the cliff.

Eventually they slowed down and reached the edge. Wind stared intently into the abyss.

"What are you looking for?" Krieg thought.

"Wait," Wind replied. "I cannot believe I live to witness this."

There was suddenly a gust of icy wind coming from deep below and going through them. It seemed as if the wind up here answered and another gust reached them, this time from inland.

"It is happening!" Wind could not contain her joy.

"What is it?" Krieg asked.

"Look!"

At that moment the depths below them began to glow. The fog covering most of Hollow's Gate became illuminated from underneath in golden light. It was a magnificent sight. Then the fog and clouds in the middle of the large Hollow began to move away and toward the edge. Small beams of light broke through the fog until they became one single beam that reached high into the night sky. When Krieg looked at Wind he saw her face reflecting the light from below. He knew at that moment that they were about to witness something extraordinary, something he couldn't even begin to understand.

"The beacon has been activated. The sky people will rise up into the heavens once more. I thought I'd never witness this again." She began to weep.

For a while, nothing happened. And then Krieg saw it. More shadows than actual forms, he saw what looked like people, dozens of them. Each of them seemed to sit on a bar that was connected by thin strings to a large sphere that looked like glass. They slowly floated upward toward the sky inside the beacon of light.

"These are my people."

"Your people?" Krieg asked.

"Will you believe me when I tell you that many centuries ago Pegasus and sky people lived in a city down in the Deep together as equals?"

Both watched as the figures floated up into the night sky until they disappeared.

"Krieg, I do not want you to be in the unknown about your friends any longer. Something is happening here that I do not yet fully understand but I am quite certain it has to do with your arrival."

"Our arrival?" Krieg asked.

"Yes. And the odd thing is that you, none of you, are mentioned anywhere in any prophecy or scripture or even folk tales. It is as if you were not supposed to happen, that you were not supposed to find each other but you did. Extraordinary things happen when ordinary folk begin to imagine the unthinkable."

"I don't understand. We just got here because we were pursued by a pack of hyenas. We almost fell over the edge. I almost got killed by my captures five days past. We were just lucky to be alive…"

"Luck has nothing to do with anything, Krieg. There is no such thing. It is something we invented to keep the power of our own mind at bay. It was not luck that you have found me. It was not luck that the beacon has been activated. I do not know what happened to your friends, Krieg, but I will go and find out and if they are alive I will find them."

There was a pause where she looked at him.

"I should go now."

With that she walked back from the edge.

"Now?" Krieg asked.

"I need a hundred yards," she said.

"Wind, how do you know that you can still fly?" Krieg asked.

"I don't." She replied. "But there is only one way to find out."

She went back further.

"Don't you want to wait a little longer? Just to be sure?" Krieg realized that his concern was not only for her. What about him? What if she didn't come back? There was no way for him to get down below. He was also concerned about what Wind would find down there. Whatever was left of Joshua and the wolf, if there was anything left. He felt trapped.

Wind was about a hundred yards away from the cliff when she turned around to face the edge.

"Be careful," he told her.

"I will be. Will you wait here until I'm back?"

"I don't know. I'm not sure what I'm going to do."

She looked at him for a moment.

"I think you do," she answered.

And with that she jumped forward, both front hooves in the air, then raced with powerful strides toward the edge.

"Your limitations, Krieg," he heard her in his thoughts as she approached the edge. "They only exist in your mind. Free them and be free."

She jumped. Krieg followed her and watched her jump off the sheer drop and disappear. When he reached the edge she was already far down. His heart stopped for a moment out of fear for her but then he saw her wings unfold and the upward winds take her, transporting her almost back to his height. She pushed her wings down and flew past him only to dive again. He could sense her immense joy.

"I remember!" Her ecstatic thoughts told him. "I remember it, Krieg."

He stood at the edge of the sheer drop, looking down and he felt something that he had felt only once since his days of the Great War: It was fear. It paralyzed him, made his mouth dry and made his heart beat against his chest.

"Be free!" The faintest thought reached him while he watched her disappear into the clouds. "Be yourself and be free…"

He looked down into the deep for a while longer letting everything that he felt wash through him, take over and envelop him completely. Then he trotted about a hundred yards back from the edge and turned around. This was it. He would do this or die. The thought of the inevitability of his choice let everything around him quiet down. Without hesitation he jumped forward and began to gallop, concentrating only on his hooves racing over the ground carrying him toward the edge, toward either life or death. Thirty yards to go. He had reached his maximum speed. His powerful muscles pushed him further and further. Twenty yards. He could see the edge clearly before him coming ever closer.

Ten yards. He reached the point of no return. There was nothing stopping him. And with that thought he jumped.

He fell much faster than he had imagined he would. He had no frame of reference for falling this deep, this far. Back at the waterfall he had gotten a small inkling. But this was a five thousand foot drop.

"Just let it happen," he thought to himself. "Just let it happen."

Having reached terminal velocity at fifty four yards per second he had the strange sensation of hovering even though the sound of the wind was deafening in his ears. He could not see anything and part of him waited for the inevitable crash when he would hit the ground. Then he broke through the clouds and for a split second he saw Hollow's Gate far below him and its beauty took his breath away. And then everything went black.

9. Eagles

Suddenly the ground beneath them gave way and, at first, Joshua thought that Krieg and the Pegasus, together with the cliff behind them, moved away from him. But then he realized that he and Grey were moving away from them! At that moment he knew what the cracking sound was. A large part of the plateau on which they stood was breaking off, taking him and the wolf with it and disappearing into the depth below. And then he fell.

His immediate concern was for the wolf. "Grey!" He thought frantically as he saw the wolf try desperately to hold on to something and then slide off the breaking rock and fall. Joshua knew at that moment that there was nothing he could do for the wolf. He would never reach him even though he tugged his wings in as much as he could in an attempt to somehow get close to him. The wolf's weight made him fall much faster than Joshua. He saw him for an instant far below and Joshua thought at that moment that his heart would break. Then the wolf disappeared into the fog and was gone. Out of the corner of his eye Joshua saw the Pegasus break free and the path they came on beginning to crumble. Suddenly there were large rocks flying toward him and his only choice was to unfold his wings and fly, moving away from the falling rocks.

When his wings unfolded and he flew away from the cliff, he saw the Pegasus and Krieg running along the path as it broke off underneath them. They made it just in time to the second path that lead upward. For a split second Joshua considered flying back toward Krieg but he realized that he would never make it up there again. Then the fog enclosed him and he didn't see anything anymore. He could hear the wind under his wings but as he made small adjustments, he sailed in almost complete silence. In the distance he heard the rocks breaking off the cliff in an eerie sound as the path to the waterfall crumbled. Then this too quieted down until there was no more sound at all. For a while, Joshua felt suspended as if in a no man's land feeling nothing but the wind under his wings.

Then he broke through the fog and as he looked down he saw Hollow's Gate far below. It was unlike anything he had ever seen. From up here he could see shades of green interspersed with dark indentations. There was a large area to the west that looked like ancient ruins, geometrical patterns of dark color within the shades of green. He saw two great lakes to the southwest that looked like tears of deep indigo, and a massive ice formation reaching up the sheer cliffs in tongs of silver. Just as he began to wonder why he couldn't see any sign of the falling wolf, everything suddenly went black.

* * *

…And then there was nothingness. Joshua felt like he was suspended in complete darkness. He wasn't even sure if he was still flying, so still was the air around him. He experienced himself as both tiny, no bigger than a grain of sand, and simultaneously stretched out and completely encompassing the whole world. It was as if his mind expanded many fold in all directions reaching deep into the earth and far into vast space. He knew at that moment with absolute certainty that there was more to him than feathers and skin and bones. But before he could even think about this and as suddenly as the blackness came, it went, and Joshua found himself back in the air over Hollow's Gate.

After reorienting himself, he decided to fly as close to the cliff as possible. Maybe there was a fighting chance he could see the wolf somewhere. Part of him was horrified of finding his friend and wished he would be spared having to look at him. He wanted to keep Grey in his memories as he had known him, not as he would see him with his body broken somewhere at the bottom of Hollow's Gate. Another part wished he would still be alive somehow but that option seemed completely impossible right now.

It was strange to fly along the massive cliff that spanned from the surface high above all the way down to the bottom, a straight five thousand foot drop. The rock was smooth and had almost no cracks or indentations of any kind in it. From here Joshua could see the cliffs stretching in both directions meeting in a perfect circle far in the distance. The sheer size of it was stupendous. He couldn't escape the feeling that the circular shape was not a natural phenomenon and that this place was in fact created, formed by something other than what natural laws would allow—a force more powerful than anything he could imagine.

Eventually he landed. Where the ground met the straight cliff wall, it sloped upward in a gentle curve until the soil touched the stone. It was as if the earth here had been pushed toward the cliff and up at least fifty feet. When he found his bearings, Joshua decided to walk along the cliff for a while, hoping to find his friend and at the same time hoping not to find him at all.

As he walked along the massive wall, he couldn't help but feel smaller and smaller, almost insignificant, as if everything he had done and everything that he was amounted to nothing in the end. He had lost his new found friends almost as soon as he had found them. He was at the bottom of an abyss that seemed to hold no hope for ever getting back to the surface. And even if he were to reach it, what then? Emptiness spread within him and he could not remember ever having felt so alone. He walked for hours and lost all sense of time, his thoughts caught in an endless spiral of despair from which he could not escape. That's why he didn't hear it at first.

So deeply immersed was he in his own world that it took him a few moments before the eagle's cry reached him. He only started hearing it when he heard the second sound: the howling of a wolf. It couldn't be that far away. It sounded eerie at first but then, before he saw them physically, he saw them in his mind. And what came with the image was the sound of laughter. It was laughter that brought with it the glad realization that the wolf was alive, and Joshua couldn't help but jump up and fly the last distance before he came around a large rock and saw them.

Wolf and eagle sat next to each other on a moss covered rock. The eagle was an impressive bird as it was about the same size as the large wolf. Grey gave out howls that, under different circumstances, would have been bone chilling to Joshua. The eagle let out long cries and throughout that, Joshua could hear their laughter in his mind. First he was stunned, watching them in disbelief. Then he couldn't help but join in. He laughed long and hard and the joy of having found his companion safe and sound swept over him and he laughed until he sank to the ground.

"Tidings of a red rooster and his companions searching for the cave of dreams have reached us in the deep." The eagle's thoughts stood in Joshua's mind and for a moment he felt as if he was lifted up high into the heavens, soaring there.

"You know of us?" Joshua replied.

"Yes we do. Sometimes legends become legends while they happen," the eagle answered. "There has not been anyone searching for the cave of dreams within this lifetime and many before that one. The freeing of the Pegasus has set in motion an infinite number of possibilities that did not exist before. But be wary. There are forces at work here, my red friend, that will try to stop you from ever reaching your goal and there are forces here and inside the mountain that will do whatever it takes for you not to find what you are looking for."

"So, it is real?" Joshua was surprised about his own question. Did he not think his dream would have a chance to become reality? He had to admit to himself at that moment that, for a while now, he did not really believe in his dreams anymore and that he had mainly been on this journey because of his companions.

"That's why they are with you," the eagle interrupted his stream of thought. "They are with you to keep your dream alive within you. Do not abandon it. Do not give in, whatever may occur. Hollow's Gate, the Great Deep, is what you must conquer in order to reach the entrance to Storm Mountain, the entrance to the dark. For you must first face your nightmares before you can reach the cave of dreams."

With that, the eagle jumped off the rock and landed in front of Joshua. He was easily four times Joshua's size with white feathers around his massive beak and down his chest and light brown wings with dark edges. His eyes, Joshua felt, could see deep into his soul. He was in awe of the eagle but at the same time had the strange sensation that this awe was reflected back to him.

"Ayres greets you." The eagle opened his wings and when Joshua thought he would take flight, he bowed his head deep before Joshua. Then he pushed off the ground and with a few powerful strokes of his wings, he was already high up in the air where he began to circle overhead, crying out several times.

Joshua, stunned and somewhat embarrassed, looked in disbelief from the eagle to the wolf who jumped down from the rock and came toward him.

"I'm so glad you are alive," Joshua couldn't contain his joy. "How did you… how is it possible that you live? And what in all the world does this all mean?"

"Come," the wolf replied. "Let's find some water and food and I will tell you everything I know."

As they walked through the green pasture that was dotted with large trees with branches wide and low to the ground, Joshua wondered how he had heard that Hollow's Gate was a dark place filled with creatures who avoided the light. What he saw now was a lush landscape with hills and valleys and—"

"Do not be deceived by its beauty," Grey brought him back. "It is a place of trials and tribulations and its laws are completely its own. A day lasts seven days but one night lasts as long and you want to be as far away from here as possible when the sun sets in the eastern sky."

"How did you survive?" Joshua asked.

As the wolf looked at him Joshua began to see an image of Grey falling through the sky like a stone. He passed through the fog and when the blackness came, for an instant there were memories of the wolf's companion at his side roaming the ice forests in deep winter. The sting of loss the wolf felt at that moment lingered in Joshua's mind like an echo deep inside him. Then the blackness was gone and the ground came closer and closer until suddenly there was a pull and a piercing pain in the wolf's sides. Joshua saw the eagle with the wolf in his talons gliding down toward the ground.

"Did the eagle see you?" Joshua asked. "How could he see you and fly down to catch you so fast?"

"It has to do with the Gate of Time," Grey replied.

"The Gate of Time?" Joshua asked.

"Time down here flows slower than on the surface. A week down here is but a day above. The Gate of Time lies in the middle between the two worlds. It is an area you pass through to reach the bottom. It is an area where time does not exist, where the past and the future are equally balanced in the present."

"I'm not sure I understand," Joshua must have shown his confusion for Grey stopped and turned toward Joshua.

"The eagles have their nests right below the Gate. They see through it and beyond. When I fell, Ayres saw me coming toward it. But because time flows differently above it, he saw me as if I fell very slowly. He recognized me and when I passed through the Gate, he caught me and brought me safely to the ground."

"How do you know him?" Joshua asked.

"That, my friend, is a long story and one I am more than willing to share—after we eat."

And that was that. They walked a little further to a place where water ran over a few large rocks to create a small pool at the bottom. Grey left for a while to look for game. The earth around the pool was soft and there were berry bushes at the edge of the water. Joshua, for the first time in days, could still his hunger completely. And weren't there the nagging concern for Krieg and what was to become of him, he would have been content.

10. Mirrors

"You don't have to hide your food from me," Joshua thought to the wolf when he came back. "I don't mind you eating in front of me. You can't be different than what you are."

"And you can't help feeling uneasy. So, I eat away from you and then I come back," the wolf replied.

Joshua, as usual, could not escape the wolf's logic. He knew better by now not to argue especially when it was clear that Grey was right.

"I have so many questions," Joshua thought.

"I'm sure, in time they will be answered," Grey thought back. "But what of Krieg and the Pegasus?"

"Last I saw, they had reached the steep path that lead to the surface. I know nothing beyond that," Joshua answered.

"At least they are safe for now, it seems," the wolf thought.

But his concern betrayed him and Joshua knew that this was a mere hope the wolf held and not a certainty. For a while there was silence between them and all they heard was the chirping of the insects and the soft breeze rustling the tree tops and the grasses in the fields.

"How do you know this place?" Joshua wasn't so sure if he wanted to know the answer but he asked it anyway.

"I don't. At least I don't remember. Wolves and eagles have always formed close bonds with each other throughout the ages. I have known

Ayres since I was a cub. We both came from the Ice Forests and in our youth there was a time when we hunted the great white tundra together. No game was too big for us. There were huge buffalo that provided food for a moon for both our families. Once we left the days of our youth behind, Ayres answered the call to become the Guardian of the Gate. He has lived down here since then. It is a solitary life but one that can bring great joys to those who fully embrace it. Sometimes what I believe to be my own memory turns out not to belong to me, but to him. But it is clouded and inaccessible most of the time. Once in a while I get a glimpse into what I know are not my own thoughts, but the eagle's.

"It looks like you have questions of your own," Joshua thought to the wolf.

"I do indeed," the wolf answered.

There was a pause when Joshua looked at the wolf. He saw something in his eyes that at first he thought not to speak to him about again.

"Grey."

"Yes."

"You think about your companion often, don't you?" Joshua realized that he probably should have left it alone but now it was too late to take it back. "You don't have to say anything, I'm sorry. I didn't mean to burden you with my questions."

Grey looked at him. "I think of her all the time, Joshua. I think of her when I first awake and when I go to sleep at night. I see her in the water and in the clouds in the sky. I see her everywhere. And yet, she seems so far away and unreachable and sometimes I think not to live if I were to continue to live without her."

"I'm sorry."

"Do not be, for you are a good friend and friends like you are harder to find than you think. It soothes my pain and helps so it does not devour me from the inside and feed on itself."

They looked at each other for a moment longer. Then Grey let out a long yawn and slumped to his side. Joshua looked up into the sky. He realized that there were neither clouds nor fog. Strange, as from above you could not see down here at all. And while he wondered why this was, he suddenly became very tired and he fell into a dreamless sleep from which he woke with the sun in his face, warming his feathers.

* * *

When he opened his eyes, disoriented at first, Joshua saw a shimmering in the distance as if the light and air played a trick on his eyes.

"Grey," he thought as he couldn't see the wolf anywhere.

He looked around. All was quiet. The image of a clear brook came into his mind with the wolf jumping in looking for fish until he finally caught one. That's when Grey came around a small hill toward him. When he arrived he shook himself, spraying water everywhere. Joshua smiled in his thoughts.

"How far away do you think this is?" Joshua looked in the direction of the shimmering air.

"About two days, maybe three. Hard to tell from here. If we climb further up somewhere, we might get a better idea," the wolf answered.

"Maybe we should go there," Joshua thought.

"What makes you think that?" Grey answered.

"I don't know," Joshua replied. "Probably because I don't know where else to go."

"Sometimes what's right in front of you is where you should go," the wolf thought.

"And sometimes it's just the opposite," Joshua answered.

"I guess we'll find out soon enough."

They didn't know for how long they had walked but as they crossed fields of green and gold glistening in the sun and small creeks that lead into a marsh land and beyond, the sheer cliffs behind them fell further and further away. When the sun had reached the zenith, they climbed a small hill to find an area to rest in. Joshua's inner clock was completely out of sorts. They must have been travelling for a few days at least, even though the sun had never set and was just today reaching its midpoint. As they looked down from the hill into the vast valley below, they saw the shimmering in the distance as if hundreds and hundreds of mirrors reflected the light and landscape around them, projecting it infinitely into one another.

By their estimation they were still a day's journey away but as they walked down the hill and continued toward it they began to see two figures, about a half mile ahead of them, coming in their direction. They realized at some point that they were walking toward themselves. Joshua could make out his red colored shape shimmering in the sun. He saw the wolf next to himself and he saw the cliffs behind them far in the distance. He knew suddenly that he was looking into a tremendous mirror—at least twenty stories high and as wide.

"What is this?" Joshua asked.

"I do not know," Grey answered.

Joshua, at that moment, had a strange and unsettling thought. "What if there is nothing behind this and all that we have been looking at this whole time was a reflection of ourselves and whatever lay behind us."

"I hope you are wrong but I can't escape the feeling that you might be right." Grey could not hide the concern in his thoughts. "Let us be careful."

As they came closer Joshua couldn't shake the feeling of uneasiness that had crept up inside him. "I don't like this. I don't like this at all," he thought to Grey. And then, in the mirror image, he saw the wolf bare his teeth and suddenly and without any warning grab Joshua's neck between his massive fangs. Joshua let out a cry as he flew up in the air, realizing that what he saw in the mirror was not what had happened. Grey was as surprised as Joshua.

"Did you see that?" He asked.

"No. I just saw you fly up in the air suddenly," the wolf replied.

"I saw in the mirror that you suddenly went after my throat…" The horror of the thought let Joshua pause.

"Joshua." The wolf stopped and looked at him. "You must know that I would never do that."

"I do know it, Grey."

"Do you?"

Joshua realized that as sure as he wanted to be that his friend would never turn on him, he really wasn't. There was always a small doubt in him as if he never could fully trust Grey, that he had to hold back and keep part of himself safe somehow by not completely giving himself over to his friend. Otherwise he wouldn't have had a reaction such as the one he just had.

"Do you really ever know anybody?" Joshua didn't realize how strongly he suddenly thought this to be true. What could have ever made him trust a wolf? As he thought this, he saw his mirror image suddenly split into two and he realized that they had reached the entrance.

"Are you sure you want to go inside?" Grey asked.

"No. But I do not believe there to be much choice. Do you?"

As the wolf looked at him, there was a foreboding in his eyes, as if both knew that whatever it was they would encounter on the other side of that mirror, would test the bindings of their friendship to the breaking point.

When they entered, it was as if the small opening disappeared behind them. It wasn't so much that it was gone but rather it was multiplied and multiplied again so that it was impossible to see which one was the real entrance and which one was its mere mirror image. The ground they stood on was stone, deep black and polished swallowing light rather than reflecting it.

"Where should we go?" Joshua asked.

"Your guess is as good as mine," the wolf answered gravely.

As they walked away from where they thought the entrance had been, Joshua looked up. There was a mirror on each side of the narrow walkway as high as he could see. He saw himself next to the wolf half in the shadows and thought suddenly about the hens back in the coop as they went about their day. He thought about them pecking the ground, eating grass or just sitting in the sun… Until death came to claim them and he saw them die right in front of him. But in his vision it suddenly wasn't an owl that took them, but a wolf. His eyes were red and his blood smeared snout snapped their little necks one by one. The image was visible in the mirror across from him. He saw the coop and the pen right there in front of him and he saw the wolf wreak havoc among his flock.

"NO!" He shouted in his thoughts. "Get away from them! Leave them alone!"

"Joshua!" The wolf's shout brought him back.

The vision disappeared as quickly as it came and what was left was the wolf next to him in the mirror.

"Why did you leave them, Joshua?" The wolf thought to him.

"What do you mean?"

"Why did you leave your flock when you knew they would be in danger because of it?" The wolf looked at him coldly across the mirror. Joshua knew he was right. Deep down that's what he had been thinking since this journey began. Joshua walked very close to the mirror and looked at his image. He saw himself strutting in front of the hens, proud and cocky and he hated himself for it. How could he ever have had any respect for himself? He saw now that he was the lowest of the low. He saw himself puny and ugly and he detested what he saw. So much so that he had to look away and close his eyes, appalled by his image.

"You do not deserve to live," the wolf's thoughts stood in his mind. As he opened his eyes, he saw the wolf walking next to him. When he looked into the mirror Grey's image was distorted—a mask of terror with long fangs for teeth, red eyes and a low growl coming from him.

Then an opening appeared suddenly, leading into another hallway perpendicular to this one. For a moment they stood there unsure which way to go.

"I think we should go straight," Grey thought.

"I think this way is better," Joshua pointed through the opening. Neither of them moved. "Maybe… it would be best if we were to continue… on our own." Joshua thought.

"I don't think that's such a good idea. We should stay together," the wolf answered. "I think we have a better chance of surviving this if we don't split up."

Joshua heard the wolf clearly in his thoughts. But behind it he heard laughter. The wolf's mocking laughter as if to tell him that if they were to stay together it would be clear as to who would survive this and who wouldn't.

"I'm going this way," Joshua heard himself think and to his surprise he stepped into the opening and walked away.

After a while he turned around but the wolf was gone. Why did he walk away? He suddenly couldn't understand his reasoning. All seemed so clear just minutes ago. His friend had betrayed him. He had shown him his real self behind the mask of friendship. Betrayed him? He couldn't even fathom the thought of it right now. He never thought that before and certainly didn't think it now. Something strange was going on here.

"Grey! Grey?" He thought into the empty corridor. Suddenly he felt trapped. Better to go back. He turned around and went back to where he came from, where he thought the opening should be. But he must have walked for a good fifteen minutes before he realized that he might have passed it. He turned around again watching both sides of the mirrored walls for an opening. To his surprise, after only a few minutes the hallway ended into yet another corridor. "That can't be right," he thought.

As he looked down the long hallway it became clear to him that he was lost. He had no sense of where he was or where to go. "Grey, where are you?" He doubted that his thoughts reached the wolf.

"Grey!" Even his own thoughts seemed to have an eerie echo in here.

Without waiting for an answer Joshua began to walk. The last thing that would help him and his friend was for him to just wait here. As he walked over the cold black stone he tried as much as he could to follow his instinct as to where to go and where to turn. He realized that the labyrinth was much bigger than he had envisioned. After what he thought an eternity he suddenly saw something far on the other side of yet another seemingly endless corridor. His pace quickened for he thought it some kind of a sign of where to go next. But when he came closer he saw that it was a skeleton. A small animal, maybe a fox or something similar. Its bones were pushed to one side and up against the mirror as if searching for comfort in death.

Up until now Joshua was hopeful to find a way out, but this small hope faded fast. "I'm going to die in here," he thought to himself. A sense of desolation washed over him at the realization that his death would probably not be an easy one. He could make it another day or maybe two without water but then he would begin to weaken and soon he would have to lie down and finally just wait until death would claim him.

* * *

The howling was so loud he could have sworn it was right next to him. Completely startled he let out a crow.

"Where are you?" Grey's thoughts reached him faintly. He couldn't remember having ever felt something so comforting in his life.

"I'm here. I'm right here!" He answered. For an instant he saw the wolf's image in his mind. Then, through the wolf's eyes, he saw in the mirror the wolf's companion walking toward him. Just before she reached Grey, an arrow penetrated her side and she died. Then the howling started again.

"Grey, try not to think of her."

"I can't!" The wolf answered in agony.

Joshua saw the same sequence over and over again in his mind.

"Stay there! I'll try to come to you," Joshua felt the wolf's pain and fueled by that he ran and flew down the corridor looking for a way to get to the wolf. He made two right turns, certain he had remembered correctly where he was in relation to before. But after two more turns and a dead end, he had lost it again. He kept going, running down long corridors, making turn after turn after turn. Sometimes he thought he saw something far ahead but when he got there it was just his own mirror image in a dead end.

He wandered the endless labyrinth for close to a day. Once in a while he heard the distant howling of the wolf. His heart broke for him and he let out his own rooster crows that echoed eerily through the dark corridors. If they ever reached the wolf he did not know it. In the end he just sank to the ground, exhausted and overwhelmed by the hopelessness of it all. He looked at himself in the mirror, looked at his face, his eyes, his beak. He saw the colors of his tail feathers and the red coloring of his back and wings. He just sat there staring at himself in the mirror for a long time.

The thought came slowly as if approaching from deep inside. It was quiet at first and small. But it gained momentum and at one point Joshua became aware of it.

"There must be a way out."

Faint still but persistent, the thought grew in strength, and as it grew in strength it grew in hope as well. And suddenly a second thought joined the first.

"We can't die in here."

And when this one began to reach his awareness he knew he had to find it in himself to get up.

"Get up." He thought to himself.

"Get up!" He thought to his mirror image.

"Get UP!"

And then he could no longer dismiss it. He had but one choice—to follow it.

He stood up, let the wave of dizziness wash over him; let the fear and hopelessness take him and pass through him. And then he knew it. There was just no way he would let his friend die. He had to find a way out.

He began to run. He ran down the corridor, not thinking at all what would be the right opening, the right direction to take at any of the cross roads. He just ran what appeared to be a zigzag through the massive labyrinth. Twice he heard distant howling but he kept running. Until suddenly he stepped into nothingness. The floor was gone. By sheer instinct he opened his wings and flew across to what looked like a platform in a large dome like structure that had mirrors only on its sides leaving a large empty space in the middle.

"This must be the center where all the corridors lead to," he thought to himself. But there was something else. He was missing something. He couldn't pinpoint it but he was sure he just missed a crucial piece of information. Before he could follow the thought he suddenly saw the large image of a female wolf on one of the mirrors. She looked past him into one of the corridors. When Joshua followed her gaze he saw Grey on the far side of a corridor. At first he couldn't make out what was happening but then he saw that the wolf ran toward the image. In full speed and with long strides he raced down the corridor toward Joshua…

"NO! Grey, NO!" He screamed in his thoughts while letting out a crow. Out of sheer desperation he flew up in the air and toward the wolf. He made it across the gap to the other side noticing the low glowing remnants of animal bones deep down.

"Grey, stop!" Joshua ran and flew toward Grey who just now seemed to notice Joshua.

"THEREISABIGWHOLEINTHEGROUNDYOUHAVETO STOP!"

Joshua saw the wolf react to his plea and try to stop his momentum. But the stone was too slippery and both realized that he would not be able to stop himself in time.

"You have to jump!" Joshua yelled in his thoughts while flying up in the air and letting the wolf run under him and toward the large gap. As he turned his head in the air he saw Grey gaining speed again and jumping…

All went quiet in Joshua at that moment. It was as if time stood still. Joshua saw the wolf stretch himself in the air to bridge the gap. He saw his gray coat with two of his paws being almost white. He saw his ears flat against his head and his teeth bared but what he saw beyond this was the wolf's undying wish to live, to fulfill his promise to his companion to live a full life, to be ALIVE.

At that moment, Joshua was suddenly overcome by a fierce love for the wolf and for all that he was. It was a love reaching from brother to brother bridging the gap between them and enveloping both. And what he felt he could not contain any longer. He let out a crow that carried with it all that he felt at that moment—all his beliefs, all of himself, his past, his present and what he wished to become.

As he cried out, he saw the mirrors move. Not move as such but rather bend. As if a pebble fell into a still lake, the mirrors suddenly had waves in them extending from within toward the outside. And as the wolf landed on the other side of the gap, the mirrors—ALL the mirrors—imploded with a deafening sound. Joshua flew across the gap and while he did, myriads of tiny particles fell to the ground creating a cacophony of sound of shattering glass.

When Joshua landed on the other side he suddenly realized the missing piece of information he could not remember before. The large dome had no ceiling. The night sky illuminated the shattering glass creating a myriad of reflections of star light. Joshua and the wolf watched as the glass particles hit the ground but instead of spreading they began to liquefy almost instantly. Where the mirrors had stood there were now channels. All the pieces of the mirrors flowed into them. The substance had the color of silvery glass, reflecting the moon light high above and emitting a golden glow.

All was suddenly quiet. There were geometrical patterns of the low glowing light in the ground as far as they could see, tracing the footprint of the massive labyrinth that stretched out far into the night. Joshua and the wolf were awestruck. It took them several minutes to process what had happened. They stood, shaking, in the middle of the platform, barely able to grasp what was happening. The beauty in the pattern of the emitting light stood in stark contrast with the utter danger they had barely escaped.

"We made it," the wolf thought. "I don't know how but we made it. Whatever you did, it worked."

"I didn't really do anything," Joshua replied.

"Yes, you did. You stopped me from falling to my death. The pain of seeing my beloved companion die over and over again made me blind to anything except her image."

Joshua could see the anguish still lingering in the wolf's eyes.

"I'm just glad it's over," Joshua thought.

"Me too," Grey answered.

"Then let us leave this place and let us go right now," Joshua replied.

"Agreed," Grey answered.

As they looked around they saw a path of black stone to the northwest leading across the large gap which was now entirely filled with liquid glass. As they crossed it, Joshua wondered how many animals had lost their lives down there over time.

They decided to follow the widest channel as it seemed to lead out of the maze. As they walked, the smaller channels began flowing into the larger one until they found themselves outside the geometrical patterns on another path made of the same black stone. The liquid glass flowed next to it emitting a golden glow that reached a short distance past them into the darkness and to the edge on the other side of the path they walked on. As they traveled through the night, they could make out the dark silhouettes of hills on both sides against the night sky. Occasionally the stone path came close to large boulders of moss covered rock. The boulders had strange shapes that were reminiscent of serpent's heads. Sometimes Joshua could make out the shapes of long snake like bodies that were connected to the heads. They must have been here for eons, half buried into the hills. Ancient guardians of the path they walked on.

It was impossible to look deeper into the night as the glow around the path made the darkness beyond it impenetrable. But after a while, Joshua could sense, almost feel, something lurking behind the veil of light.

"Grey."

"Yes, I can feel it too."

"What do you think it is?"

"I'm not sure. But whatever it is that waits beyond the veil is not on our side.

After a while they came to the end of the flowing river of glass. It moved slightly slower than Joshua and the wolf had walked. The light reached about ten feet into the night ahead. There they could make out the dark silhouettes of creatures such as Joshua had never seen or dreamed of. They seemed to change their shapes constantly as they moved along the edge of the light. It was as if they were attracted by its brightness and, at the same time, repelled by it for they could not pass through to Joshua and the wolf inside.

"If we stay within the circle of the light we should be fine," Grey thought.

"Let's hope so," Joshua thought back.

Grey, aware of the fear in Joshua's thoughts, changed places with him, taking him in the middle between the night and the channel of glass next to them. And so, under the protection of the light, Joshua and the wolf traveled for what on the surface would have been close to two days. Once in a while the channel passed small streams where they could quench their thirst. Joshua found plenty of food and Grey was able to even catch a fish or two. When they rested here and there for a couple of hours, they held watch over each other. During the times when Joshua watched over his companion's sleep, he thought back in horror to the time they spent in the labyrinth and how powerful the wolf's 'evil' thoughts appeared to him. Now he couldn't even conceive of them as being real and true. He decided then and there never to doubt the wolf again.

11. Ruins

awn came slowly and when they began to see beyond the light they realized that they had left the hills behind and had entered a forest. Large trees stood darkly against the still grey sky. Where before the channel of glass was embedded in the hills, it now followed a straight line deep into the forest. The further they went, the quieter it seemed to get. The sounds of the birds around them faded until all they heard was their own footsteps on the stone path. At one point the channel made a sudden sharp turn to the left disappearing into the trees. Without warning, the glow the liquid glass emitted suddenly stopped. For a moment, Joshua had the horrifying thought that the night creatures that had traveled with them would now come forward and take them. But they were gone. Joshua and Grey could only surmise that the emerging day light was enough to push them back to where they had come from.

A few feet away, another channel came out of the woods to the right. That one was empty. It made a sharp turn in front of them and continued straight ahead

"It seems as if the channel that leads into the woods somehow loops back on the other side," Joshua thought. "It might take a while for the liquid to come full circle and continue on its path."

"Should we follow it then?" Grey asked.

"I think we should go straight and see where it leads," Joshua thought.

"Agreed," the wolf thought back.

Now that they didn't have to use the stone path, they walked on pine needles which softened their steps, so much so, that they almost didn't hear anything at all. Joshua thought it eerie and strangely comforting at the same time.

They began to pass what looked like old stone foundations of buildings long since gone, crumbled and overgrown. Some of them had oddly shaped forms and some seemed to randomly connect to others. The further they went, the more they became certain that this must have been a city at some point in time. They realized that what they were passing by must have been buildings once—centuries, even millennia ago. Joshua had the distinct feeling that they walked on hallowed ground, on the sacred soil of an ancient civilization of which only remnants remained.

They came to a point where they could see what must have been the center of the city in the distance. The ruins formed a half circle on either side of the channel, leaving a large, round area in the middle open. At first Joshua couldn't make out what it was but as they came closer they saw a large crater in the center. Approximately fifty yards in diameter, the crater had straight walls, very similar to those surrounding Hollow's Gate. They disappeared into nothingness below. The channel here split up and continued on both sides of the crater, surrounding it and completing the loop on the other side.

Slowly, Joshua and Grey walked around the edge of the crater.

"This may sound strange," Joshua thought to the wolf, "but is it possible that we are right now exactly in the center of Hollow's Gate?"

"Why do you think that?" Grey replied.

"When we fell from the plateau, for a moment I saw those strange patterns toward the middle. It must have been the ruins of the old city we are in."

"Joshua, I didn't want to say anything but this, all of this, seems very familiar. It is as if I have walked these streets before in ancient times. It must have been one of the eagle's memories while flying overhead, as I have never been here."

"Or maybe you have," Joshua thought, more to himself than to the wolf. The whole place had a strange quality to it. As if it were permeated with something that went beyond the limits of time and space. Something so ancient he couldn't grasp it and only sense a miniscule fragment of the power it once possessed.

Across the crater, there stood the remnants of a large rectangular plate of stone. As they came closer they saw that it had signs and symbols engraved into it. Most of the upper part of the stone plate was missing, destroyed by the ages. The plate rested on a massive slab of black stone similar to the material of the path they had walked on. The symmetrical foundation of the building was in the shape of a large cathedral. This must have been some sort of place of worship. The side facing the crater was open. As they looked around, Joshua saw that all the foundations and ruins surrounding the crater were missing the wall facing it.

"What now?" He asked.

"Now we wait," Grey replied.

As they waited in silence, Joshua couldn't help but think that somehow they were witnessing something far greater than themselves. He did not yet know how the individual pieces were connected to each other and to a greater whole but deep down he could sense that something completely out of the ordinary was about to happen and that he and Grey were somehow privy to it, even part of it. The stillness of the forest, together with the quiet understanding between him and the wolf brought Joshua a sense of peace he had rarely felt and if so only for moments. This was different. It was as if peace spread within him like wings, carrying him, allowing him to feel weightless and at the same time deeply connected to the earth. In fact, at that moment there was no distinction between him and the ground he rested on, or between him and the wolf who lay only a few feet from him.

How long they sat like this Joshua couldn't tell but at some point Grey got up and looked beyond the crater into the woods.

"I can see it," he thought to Joshua.

Both watched as the liquid glass slowly flowed toward the crater. When it reached it, the glass followed the channels on either side around it and toward the point where Joshua and the wolf stood. Eventually the circle closed where both channels met. Nothing happened at first. Joshua looked down into the crater. The thought occurred to him that something was about to rise up from deep inside, something horrifying and nightmarish, and come up to the surface to take them back down with it. But nothing happened other than the strange sensation that the air began to hum slightly—a very low vibration that Joshua could feel resonating within his body.

"Do you feel that?" He asked the wolf.

There was no answer and Joshua didn't see Grey at first. Then he saw him standing in front of the broken plate of stone. They watched as the missing part of the stone plate began to rebuild itself. But not out of stone. It rebuilt itself out of light. The same happened with the walls of the building they stood in. As they looked around, they saw the walls beginning to rebuild themselves from the ground up. But where the material had been stone and wood, now it was light. Emitting a golden glow, the light took on the shape of each stone, each piece of wood, every finely crafted detail of the structure.

Joshua and Grey watched as the whole city began to rebuild itself. Doors, window sills, roof structures, even chimneys and passage ways all carved out of thin air and compressed light. Some buildings were flat and rectangular but most of them had strange shapes of half round or circular patterns. It was unlike anything Joshua had ever witnessed. There were round platforms on top of some of the roofs, the purpose of which completely eluded him.

"Joshua," Grey's thought reached him. It was barely more than a whisper, as if the wolf did not wish to disturb what was happening.

Joshua turned around facing the crater. The walls now had a slight glow to them and, as they walked toward the edge, Joshua could see far down into it. The light became brighter and brighter. Joshua and Grey, dwarfed before the large crater and only a silhouette before its immense light, stepped back to escape the blinding beam that reached far and high into the gray dawn sky. Still unable to comprehend anything they saw, they looked at each other, awed by the sheer beauty and power of what was happening. That's when they saw them.

At first, all that was visible were spheres of clear glass gently rising from deep within the crater. Then Joshua could make out small strings attached to either side of them. Not far below, the strings ended in what looked like a narrow platform. On each of the platforms sat a figure. The figures looked human but were dressed in dark body suits and masks. Some of the shapes were bigger, others smaller like children. One of the smaller figures came fairly close to Joshua and the wolf. It lifted its hand briefly to greet them in passing.

"Can you hear me?" Joshua thought to the figure. But there was no answer. He felt the figure's gaze on him until it disappeared behind another sphere that passed them. Joshua counted at least three dozen spheres, but as he looked down into the crater he saw that it must have been more than 200 spheres that ascended within the light beam into the sky. Then they were gone.

"What was that?" Joshua thought.

"I have not the slightest idea," Grey answered.

As far as they were able to see into the woods, the light structures of the city were completed. Some reached high into the sky next to the trees with wide circular stairways on the outside. Others seemed to be mere entrances to structures below the surface. There were streets and walkways and square structures that looked as if their purpose had once been to hold water. Now in their light form they were no longer remnants of an ancient past but a representation of what was still here, existing outside of time and space and reaching far beyond. As Joshua's gaze fell on the plate of stone and light within the high dome they stood closest to, they saw that there were engravings, strange markings covering the stone. When Joshua looked at them, he understood their meaning. It was as if the markings evoked images rather than mere symbols. It read:

A stream of stars forever calls you home
To where you will return
To where you still belong
The doors have long since opened
Unlocked the gates of time
The path to truth is open
The stars are now aligned
To start an ancient journey
To where you've always been
To follow your own yearning
To gather your own kin
Your fate is sealed
Your destiny is written in the sky
Your home at last revealed
You will not pass it by
And then one day the sands of time
Will vanish from your hearts
And leave no trace of them behind
Except a stream of stars.

Something stirred within Joshua. It was as if the images he saw triggered remnants of ancient memories buried deep inside, memories he could neither grasp nor put into any time frame. He realized that the meaning of what was written there could only be grasped within his heart, not with his rational mind. His rational mind, in fact, was dazzled by it. For a while longer they looked at the plate of stone. Then their eyes found each other.

"Grey?"

"Yes," the wolf answered.

"I'm thirsty." Joshua thought to him.

The wolf suddenly smiled in his thoughts.

"Then let us go and get some water. I'm ravenously hungry myself," he replied.

* * *

They decided to take one of the wider roads that lead through the city in the opposite direction from which they came. As they passed structure after structure, still stunned by the magnificent detail in the light carvings, they realized that it was no longer as quiet as it was in the center of the city. They now heard birds chirping in the distance, as if not only the city itself but its surroundings slowly awakened. The forest became lighter and the distance between the trees increased until they stood only sporadically here and there. The scenery itself changed and they entered a hilly landscape, similar to what they had traveled through during the night.

After they had been walking for a time, they suddenly saw that the road was blocked by a huge mound of earth in front of them. It was as if something had been pushed through the surface of the road and left there decades ago. The mound of earth was easily fifty feet in diameter and about twenty feet in height. Even though it was embedded into the hills it felt out of place somehow. The wolf jumped up on a ledge of rock and then walked on top of the small hill. Joshua, for some reason, stayed down. The shape of the hill reminded him of something. And before he could follow that thought further toward its origin, the mound suddenly stirred. Grey let out a howl and jumped down, joining again with Joshua.

Then the soil to the left and to the right of it was being pushed toward them revealing two massive, clawed, stump-like arms. The arms pushed themselves into the soil and then the whole hill rose up. Joshua flew back and Grey leaped away from whatever it was that began to rise. As its massive body gained about five more feet in height, earth and stones fell from its back exposing a large opening in front and a massive shell as its back. Then the head appeared. Its neck slowly extended outward toward Joshua and the wolf. It stopped only a few feet before them. They realized that they were looking at a huge turtle. Its head, waving slightly from side to side, was four times Grey's size. Its yellow eyes looked straight at them.

As Joshua glanced at the wolf he thought that he heard singing, or perhaps a sound somewhere between whistling and singing. First he thought it must have come from a bird high up in a tree. But then he realized that the sound came from the turtle. It was repeating a certain sequence of a melody over and over.

"Who are you?" The question suddenly flooded Joshua's mind and for an instant didn't leave room for anything else. Grey barked at the turtle, his teeth bared and his neck coat standing up.

"So sorry," the turtle's thoughts, now much quieter, reached them. Grey shook himself and calmed down a bit, still not quite sure what to make of this.

"I am thinking too loud. When I slept, it… I remember now… it was hard to be heard by… the others so I had to yell. I think. My apologies."

The turtle, whose massive head was still only two feet away from them, seemed to sniff them rather thoroughly.

"You could use a bath," she thought to the wolf. "And you," her head came down to Joshua's level looking straight into his eyes, only inches away from him. "You smell like adventure… But wait. You must forgive me. I can't seem to remember much of what happened, if anything. Ohhh.."

With that she slumped to the ground, creating a large dust cloud. Joshua had to turn away and for a few seconds he wasn't able to breathe. Next to him he heard Grey sneeze several times.

"So sorry, my young fellows. I'm still a bit weak in the knees… It's all somewhat hazy, you know. I must have slept… for a… very… long… time." She yawned. As she breathed out with a sigh, the wind generated from it made Joshua's feathers bend back. Grey's coat got a good airing out. So much so that he shook himself several times, while sneezing again profusely.

"I am Joshua. And this is my friend. His name is Grey. By circumstances we cannot explain we fell… from far up at the surface and somehow we ended up down here. Up there we got separated from another companion. His name is Krieg. He is possibly still there where we had freed a Pegasus from the stone before the plateau we stood on, broke off."

There was a pause during which the turtle's head swayed from left to right.

"What did you say?" The turtle asked. Joshua could sense her effort to control the volume of her thoughts.

"I said that I am Joshua. And this is my friend…"

"No. I meant… after… at the end…"

"Uhm… I mentioned my companion Krieg. He is a war horse and—"

"Pegasus. Did you say 'Pegasus'?" The turtle's thoughts were now just a whisper.

"Yes," Joshua couldn't help but whisper back to her.

"Ahh… I forgot most of what happened but it seemed to have some significance. I'm sorry. I'm not much help to you I guess. It will come to me. Give it a few years and I'll be back to my old self. But for now…," the turtle lifted her massive body off the ground again, which caused more loose earth and rocks to break off.

"…I may require some water and must make my way to the Lake of Tears. For nowhere, and I mean NOWHERE, will you find better tasting water than there. And nowhere is it clearer and colder. And nowhere can you dive deeper and still never reach the bottom."

While the turtle turned around, which wasn't a small task given her size and weight and her massive shell getting stuck in the hills that surrounded her, the melody Joshua and Grey had heard before, continued in the background going from clear high notes to a deep, low humming and then back up again.

"Can we come with you?" Joshua asked suddenly, surprised over his own question.

"Certainly," was her even more surprising answer. "It might take me a while though. Not sure how long you can wait. I don't move very fast, as you may have noticed, as long as I'm on land. But give me water.

Give me deep, fresh water. And you will see me move faster than anything in there. But you probably want to reach your destination sooner rather than later, am I right?"

"To be perfectly honest," Joshua replied, "we don't even know where to go from here."

"Ah," she answered, as she turned some more until Joshua and the wolf were suddenly looking at her rear. They glanced at each other, Grey smiling in his thoughts.

"Come on," Grey thought to Joshua as he jumped up the side of the hill and leaped down on the other side. Joshua flew up and onto the back of the large turtle. From there he flew down to stand before her again.

"If you would be so kind as to tell us which direction to go, we will be on our way," Joshua told her in his thoughts.

"The direction depends entirely on where you want to end up," she answered.

"I'm not sure," Joshua replied, "but I think we need to get into the mountain."

"Porte Des Lioness," the turtle answered. "There is an ancient entrance. Or at least there was… But you cannot find it, no. Nobody can. The glass is cracked. O I don't remember. But you must look. And wait. And wait."

"I don't understand. But maybe you can tell us where to go from here."

"Yes. I can certainly do that, my young friend. If you take this road for a while, you will come to a point where you can see a tower in the distance. Or maybe you will only see the upper most tip of it. That tower is Refuge. It stands on the edge of the great falls in the center of the Lake of Tears.

"Refuge?" Joshua asked.

"Yes," the turtle replied. "It is… a refuge. Nothing more. Nothing less. Oh… I think I… I just remembered something… Hmm… No. Sorry. It's not… It's not coming back that fast. I forgot again."

"Do you remember what it is a refuge from?" Joshua asked.

"No… YES! Wait." The turtle closed her huge eyes. Her head swayed back and forth, the melody continuing in the background.

"OH YES!… Sorry, too loud again." And she continued with a whisper, "It is because it usually gets very cold there suddenly."

"What do you mean?" Joshua asked.

"I recall a deep freeze that happens four times a year. It lasts for six hours more or less during which everything that is outside dies. You must be inside and all the way at the top of the tower… Nothing can survive being exposed to those temperatures…. I think…. Or maybe that was a dream I had. I'm really sorry I don't seem to make much sense, do I."

"It's okay," Joshua thought to her. "Thank you anyway.

"You are quite welcome, my young friend," the turtle looked at Joshua for a moment, than her head moved towards Grey.

"And you, gray one," she looked straight at the wolf. "Do not be saddened. Your companion's pain left her long ago and she is roaming the ancient hunting grounds free and much contented. Your memory has stayed with her and has not left her for a single moment since. Do not deny her presence within you for if you do, she died in vain."

When Joshua looked at Grey he saw that the wolf was stunned by what the turtle had just told him. Then the sense of relief flooding through Grey was so big that even the turtle was infected by it. Joshua was sure her laughter could be heard for miles and miles so loud were her thoughts of joy over the wolf's expression of his.

"Thank you," the wolf thought while looking up to the turtle. "I thank you. So much."

"Go now. For it will take you a good while to get to the Refuge and I can feel the cold coming deep inside my bones."

Had it become colder already? Joshua thought he had felt a rush of cold air before. Better not to waste any time.

"Farewell my young friends. Good luck on your travels and may I devote a song in your honor?"

"You may," Joshua answered.

"Two Companions in search of their destiny. I like it." The turtle closed her eyes, changed the melody into a tune with dramatic overtones.

Joshua and Grey walked away from her and around a bend in the road that lead through the hills. Just as they were about to disappear from her line of sight, Joshua caught a small fading thought.

"...Spiders."

A blast of cold air reached both of them, ruffling Grey's coat and Joshua's feathers.

"Did you hear that?" Joshua asked.

"No. What was it?" The wolf replied.

"I heard the word 'spiders'."

"Spiders? Are you sure?" Grey asked.

Whatever was left of the thought faded fast.

"I'm not sure. It probably doesn't matter." He left it at that and forgot all about it only a few minutes later.

12. Refuge

*T*hey followed the ancient road leading away from the city of light ruins and toward their next destination of which they knew very little. Both stayed within their own thoughts for the most part. Once Joshua received such a clear and strong image of the wolf's companion roaming the landscape in the ancient hunting grounds beyond the borders of this world that he could not help thinking about his own journey and the path he had taken. Not in his wildest dreams would he have been able to dream up such an adventure. He had been away from his home for less than a moon and already he had seen things that were outside the realm of experience for most of his kind. The hens and other chickens in his pen lived for their immediate surroundings, their life in the flock and mostly for the food. He could not comprehend how he had ever been satisfied with it. It was as if he did not realize what he had missed until he experienced it firsthand.

On the other side of it, he thought of all the times he had been close to death, how many dangers he had already passed through and how many more most likely awaited him on the remainder of his journey. And the outcome of it was still completely uncertain. Even if he found the feathers, what then? It was hard for him to remember how much they meant to him when they appeared in his dream. One thing was certain: if he hadn't found Grey and Krieg, he would not have come as far as he did. And even more, the friendship between them was what truly made all this worthwhile. It was more than he could have ever hoped to find.

Joshua was so deep in his thoughts, that he didn't realize the landscape had changed almost completely in the last two hours. Despite the significantly colder air, the land before them was lush and green. It felt almost tropical. Behind a hill in the distance, the upper part of the Refuge was clearly recognizable as a cylindrical structure reaching high into the sky. The visible upper part was almost completely made of glass.

The path they were on went steadily up hill and was dotted on both sides with large egg shaped boulders. Thick dark green moss grew on them. In between the oddly shaped rocks stood several trees. With their stems broad and short and their thin, long branches thickly layered with moss and algae, their bizarre shapes were reminiscent of extraordinarily large…

"SPIDERS!" Joshua's thought must have startled the wolf as he, letting out a yelp, jumped to the middle of the path and away from one of the trees. As they both looked at the trees they had to admit that there was a very close resemblance in their shape to actual spiders. Some of the trees were half buried in the ground with only their branches sticking out like thin long legs.

"They look like attack spiders." Grey's thought provoked more than mere discomfort in Joshua. In fact, he had to muster a great deal of self control in order not to follow his instincts and begin to run. As they walked past the eerie looking trees and equally disturbing egg shaped boulders, they reached the top of the hill. From here they had an unobstructed view of the Refuge. It was embedded in a magnificent landscape. With the sheer five thousand foot high wall that extended high into the sky as a backdrop, the tower, built into a massive boulder, sat near the center of a large, tear-shaped lake. The sun hitting its surface brought out the deepest cobalt blue that was reflected in the upper part of the tower which was almost completely made of glass. There was a second, similarly shaped lake behind the first one. Joshua saw large openings in the middle of each lake where the water disappeared. The path toward the lake lead through a lush green hilly landscape that was dotted with the now familiar egg shaped boulders interspersed with the strangely shaped trees. In the distance, where the land met the massive walls of Hollow's Gate, they could see what looked like tongues of ice that had crawled halfway up the sheer cliffs.

As they began their descent into the valley the wind increased, bringing ever colder air from the lakes toward them. The force of the wind gusts was so strong at times, it felt like something was pushing them back, unwilling to let them come closer. When they were half way down the hill, Joshua looked back. What he saw made his skin crawl.

"Look!" He thought quietly to the wolf.

When Grey turned around, he let out a low snarl. The coat around his neck stood up. Joshua could sense utter terror in the wolf. From here, the trees looked even more imposing, like huge spiders that were crawling out of the ground and toward them. But what they didn't see before when they walked down the hill were the small openings covered by grass and soil from one direction but now visible as holes in the ground. The holes were about six to eight yards in diameter, covering the landscape as far as they could see. There were hundreds of them.

"Joshua," Grey thought.

"Yes," Joshua answered.

"We should hurry." The wolf turned around and began to trot. Joshua had to make an active choice to turn his back to what he was looking at. Fear spread inside his chest as he started to fly and run down the path and toward the lake. The further they came the colder it got. Joshua's eyes began to tear and when they reached the shore of the lake, he couldn't feel his talons anymore. They saw a small dam built into the lake that spanned the distance between the shore and the large tower. They had about 300 yards before they reached the large boulder and then up what looked like stairs built into the rock leading to a small platform and a massive door.

Joshua heard the noise when they first stepped onto the stone dam. It was the sound of cracking ice. The lake began to freeze. The cold air suddenly hit them full force. Breathing became difficult for Joshua as they made their way across the narrow dam. He saw the edges of the lake turn into ice and the ice moving in their direction from all sides. The area where the dam met the shore was also already completely iced over and when Joshua turned his head for one second he saw that the ice extended up the hill from where they had come.

And then, suddenly, the sound of the freezing water was overpowered by yet another sound. It was the sound of hundreds and hundreds of feet crawled over a glassy surface. It was a wave of noise of otherworldly proportions coming from behind them. This time it was Grey who turned his head. What he saw was beyond anything he could possibly describe.

Out of the holes in the ground came the spiders. First dozens but then hundreds of them, their bodies covered in long hair, they came crawling with immense speed down the hill and toward the tower. They must have been three to four feet wide and at least three quarters the height of the wolf. The sound was deafening and so terrifying Joshua flew higher and faster than he ever thought he could. When they reached the other side of the dam and the stairs, the spiders had reached the ice covered lake. The wolf ran up the stone steps, taking three or four at a time. He arrived first at the plateau with the large door.

As Joshua flew up the stairs he heard the wolf in his thoughts.

"The doors, Joshua. The doors are closed. We can't get inside!"

Joshua reached the plateau. Behind him, the ice crept into the boulder. The spiders were about half way across the lake. And Joshua felt suddenly that this was it; that this was the end of his journey. It was either the spiders that reached them first or the ice. It did not matter. He didn't think his end would come like this. He was always convinced it would be from a predator, like a fox or on owl. But not a spider four times his size or temperatures that could freeze one's breath and turn it into icicles in a matter of seconds. Grey and Joshua looked at each other, for an instant wordlessly acknowledging their friendship to one another. Then they turned to face whatever it was that would reach them first.

The shadow that suddenly blocked the sun became larger and larger and Joshua looked up. Blinded by the light he saw a blurry silhouette coming toward them. He could make out a dark figure and massive wings pushing the air. And then Krieg landed next to them.

"Step back from the door," he told them in his thoughts. And before Joshua could react, the war horse kicked the door several times until it flew open.

"Get inside!" He commanded them.

And when Wind landed on the ice covered plateau, Joshua flew through the door. He was followed by Grey, Wind and Krieg.

"Go up the stair case!" Wind's thoughts reached them. "It's not over yet!"

Krieg kicked the door from the inside and it shut, the sound echoing through the large space. As Joshua ran and flew up the massive stair case that went up along the walls he heard the spiders on the outside. For a moment he took in the scenery: a wide spiral staircase of massive proportions made of stone and reaching ever higher inside the tall tower. As Krieg passed Joshua he stopped briefly.

"Fly onto my back," he told him.

Joshua did so without hesitation. As they raced up the stairs, Joshua saw the ice crawling up the walls toward them. The stone stairs far at the bottom were already completely covered. They had to reach the top of the tower before the ice overcame them completely.

"You have wings!" Joshua couldn't help but think to Krieg.

"Yes, my friend, I do."

For a brief moment, and cutting through all the fear, he felt utter joy to see Krieg alive and well. Then he looked behind him and saw that the ice had almost caught up with them.

"We're here!" Grey's thoughts reached Joshua. And with that he disappeared through an opening in the ceiling. Wind followed and then Krieg with Joshua on his back. This part of the tower was completely made of glass interlaced with thin, carefully crafted bars that made up the structure into which the glass was built. As they stood in the large space that was easily fifty yards across and at least twice as high, they could see the ice crawling up another ten yards on the glass before it stopped. At the same time the spiders reached the top of the tower. For a moment all was quiet except for the eerie crackling of the ice outside. The spider's bodies, tugged against the glass, blocked most of the light. Here and there a beam of sunlight came through the small spaces between them, illuminating parts of the floor.

The group stood huddled together in the middle of the large dome. Joshua saw that Grey's fur coat was covered in ice crystals. Parts of the wings of the Pegasus were frozen as well. And as he looked down on himself he saw that a fine layer of ice covered his feathers. They got here not a moment too soon. The joy over seeing Krieg again was overshadowed by the terrifying thought that they were surrounded by hundreds, maybe thousands, of large spiders. The relief he felt when they reached the tower room was short lived. What if the spiders found a way inside? The door at the bottom was probably still open even though Krieg tried to close it shut.

"They will not harm you." Wind's thoughts reached him like clear water bubbling to the surface of a well.

"What do you mean?" He asked.

"They will not harm you in any way. They are not here for you."

Joshua didn't understand.

"Why are they here then?" He asked.

There was a pause while Wind looked at him, her eyes kind and her presence warming his mind.

"They are here to seek shelter. The ice comes from deep within the earth, taking everything in its path. The spiders flee from it to the only place they know will save them: Refuge. If you were to look outside now you would see that none of the ones below us have survived. They all died in search of a place where the ice could not reach them. They were not after us."

"So, closing the doors killed them?" Krieg asked into the silence.

"No. Even inside, just below the floor, they would not be alive right now." Wind held Krieg's gaze. "There was nothing you could have done."

"What happens now?" Joshua asked, not sure what exactly he meant.

"Once the ice melts, the lake will take their dead. The ones that survive go back down deep into the ground."

"Until next time?" Joshua asked.

"Yes. Until next time," Wind answered.

Joshua nodded slightly. He had seen so much death in such a short period of time and each one touched him anew, each time it was as if part of himself died as well.

"Death is just a part of this world," Wind thought to him. "It is neither good nor bad. It is."

"I don't like it!" Joshua was surprised about the strength of his reaction. "Why is there life when it ends in death anyway? Why go through all this when the outcome is certain and inevitable?" Joshua was suddenly overcome by a wave of emotions of desperation, fear and a sense of loss that he couldn't comprehend.

"Joshua!" Grey's thoughts stood clear within his mind. "It's the spiders. You are experiencing what they are feeling. It is their thoughts that you are hearing."

Joshua realized at that moment that the wolf was right. He could feel it now. It was all around him. The spiders that had made it up to the top mourned the death of their brethren below. Suddenly Joshua saw the outside of the tower through their eyes. It was covered in the frozen, crystallized bodies of the spiders. One by one they fell off the ice covered walls as it began to melt. It was an image of utter horror.

"There is nothing you can do for their bodies," Wind thought to him. "But there is something you can do for us and for yourself and for them and that is that they are not excluded from our thoughts. That they are *in* our thoughts. That will accompany them to wherever they are going and to whatever awaits them next."

As Joshua thought about this, trying to comprehend what he had just heard from Wind, Krieg came over and lay down across from him and the wolf. The three of them looked at each other for a while.

"I'm so glad you are both alive," Krieg thought to them. "I was certain of your death and I felt it as my own."

"We are very glad to see you well, Krieg," the wolf replied. "Tell us what happened."

And so Krieg told the story of how he and Wind escaped the crumbling path and made it up the steep incline to the surface. He told them about the beacon and seeing the sky people float up and about himself jumping into the abyss and passing through the clouds into the blackness of the Gate of Time. When he came out of the dark he suddenly had felt a stabbing pain in his back and he realized that his fall had slowed. He became aware of his wings and began to make small adjustments to them to change direction and height. Then he saw Wind coming toward him. He felt her utter joy.

"I live!" He thought.

"Yes. And you can fly," Wind replied.

"I can fly!"

It was a feeling unlike any other he had ever experienced. He felt weightless, gliding through the air, dizzy from the sheer height and feeling the air under his wings.

"Come with me!" Wind turned toward the Wall and Krieg followed behind her. "We can use the upward winds," she thought to him and he saw her suddenly far above him. A moment later he was carried upward at least 200 yards until he was next to her again.

The exhilaration he felt was contagious and for a while both of them flew through the sky, at times gliding in almost complete silence and at others using their powerful wings to push upward. Eventually they set down in a small enclave of trees not far from the Wall to the north where the land was lush and the grass was deep green. It was warm there and the finest mist hung in the air. Moss covered the lower parts of the Wall. From high up, water ran down along it and where it hit the ground it disappeared into a narrow gap. Krieg realized that where they stood was the bottom end of the waterfall where he, Joshua and the wolf had barely escaped their fate.

"We have to find them," Krieg thought to Wind. He looked down at two half decomposed Hyenas right next to the small gap. "Even though it is the last thing I want to see, we must try to find their bodies. They should not become prey to worms and other vermin."

Wind could see the pain in Krieg's eyes.

"Then let us go and find them," Wind answered and took a few steps. "Come."

Krieg gave his silent approval and Wind began to trot and soon galloped through the trees in long strides gaining speed until she reached a large clearing and lifted off the ground. She turned in the air and flew back toward Krieg who went up on his hind legs, pushing forward and racing through the trees to the same opening. His wings unfolded and he was in the air. He gained height until they were about 200 yards above the ground.

"We should fly along the wall to the west," Wind thought to Krieg, adjusting her wings accordingly.

And so they flew along the majestic wall looking for any signs of Joshua and Grey but they couldn't find them anywhere. In the distance they saw the shimmering lights of the ruins and the beacon rising up into the sky. Krieg could sense Wind's wish to go there and stand on the ancient grounds of her city once more.

"You are right, Krieg. My home is calling for me. But answering it must wait until we have found your friends. I have waited a thousand years and I can wait a little longer."

It was then when Krieg spotted a small red dot racing across the dam and toward the Refuge. And he saw the ice closing in on them and the spiders running for their lives and he flew down and found his friends again.

13. Lioness

hen Joshua and Grey told their part of the story, Wind listened intently, asking many questions about the city of light ruins and the beacon and the engravings on the plate of stone. Joshua had many questions for Wind as well, some of which she was able to answer. She spoke about the sky people who, for centuries, visited the city through the beacon to serve the Pegasus. They lived peacefully together until some of them began to mine the mountain for rare crystals. More and more of the sky people came through the beacon and the city became a thriving mining town. But in time, most of the sky people forgot their purpose to serve the Pegasus and they began to use them in the mines. They were strong creatures and able to sustain long times without food and water deep inside the mountain. Very few of the sky people realized that they were lost. Lost in greed and the underlying despair over what they were doing to the Pegasus. Some of the sky people began to oppose. Many lost their lives in their attempts to free the Pegasus from the mines.

And one day, a small group of sky people who still believed in their purpose and that of their ancestors, destroyed the beacon, fully knowing that they would not be able to ever get back home. They fled deep into the ground. Without the beacon, the creatures of the dark came by night to take whoever was not able to find shelter. Without the beacon, the ice was able to reach far into the city and one day whoever was still above ground was prey to its deathly claws. Many died. The Pegasus that were still alive and weren't killed by the dark ones, abandoned the crumbling city. Without the beacon there was no longer any purpose for being there. And without the beacon, the city began to fall. The sky people that were left swore never to let this happen again.

Deep below the surface, they found stone plates filled with symbols of the knowledge of an ancient civilization; the one who had built the beacon in the first place. It was there were they found instructions to close the entrance to the mines; seal the Porte Des Lioness and build the labyrinth of mirrors that would allow only one with a true heart and certainty of purpose to reactivate the beacon and give the sky people another chance…

Joshua suddenly found himself back in the dark tower room realizing that everyone was looking at him.

"What are you looking at me for? I didn't do anything," he thought. "It obviously couldn't have been me. I'm certainly not true in my heart and also not at all certain of my purpose. It must be you, Grey."

The wolf smiled in his thoughts. So did Krieg and Wind.

"What?" Joshua thought. "Let me explain to you why it couldn't have been me. First of all, pure of heart I'm certainly not. I have abandoned my fellow chickens and with that sentenced them to death for which I am responsible. My heart is anything but pure. It is the opposite. And since I have found you I have pushed you into an ordeal that almost cost you your lives. Several times over. So, don't tell me that I'm anything but what I am: nothing."

Joshua looked at his friends and could not understand why they didn't agree with him.

"Grey, am I not right? You almost lost your life twice now, actually three times if you count the labyrinth. And you Krieg, I…" Joshua seemed to have lost the thread of his arguments.

"You mean you didn't save me?" Krieg thought to him. "You didn't stand up to three men who would have definitely killed me right there? You weren't the one saving us in the Great Falls?

"Krieg, I... that wasn't... I didn't save you. It was the wolf and then you saved us from the men and without the wolf I would be dead and without you I would be dead and—"

"Joshua," Wind's thoughts came to him like a warm ray of sun on a cold and dreary day. "Perfection was never necessary. Willingness was. And of that you have plenty. Your heart is open and that is all. Mistakes cannot stop you from finding your destiny. And in searching for your own you are finding it for others. You began this journey for yourself. But you will end it for everyone."

Joshua was stunned. He never thought this, never held such lofty ideas about himself. And even though Wind's thoughts were like balm on his soul, he could only accept them partially, and with many reservations. He could not believe they would ever become his only truth. There was just no way. He was who he was and accepting himself as more than that was something he could only see in others and not himself. He could see greatness in Krieg. He could see greatness in Grey and certainly in Wind. But whatever it was that grew within himself, it was safer not to go anywhere near it.

* * *

At first, Joshua wasn't aware of the shifting patterns of light and shadow on the floor. Then he saw the bodies of the spiders stir and suddenly move downward. As if compelled by an invisible force, they left behind the safety of the Refuge to return to their home deep underground. With the spiders gone a magnificent landscape revealed itself. To the north the city of light ruins shimmered through the large pines. The path into the city, past the large egg-shaped boulders and spider trees, now had taken on a completely different meaning. There was no more fear in Joshua. Just wonder. To the west and beyond the receding ice, the Great Wall of Hollow's Gate went straight up into the sky.

Joshua walked over to the southern facing side of the dome. As he approached the glass wall, he realized how high up the tower room was. Far below him, the surface of the Lake of Tears shimmered in shades of dark blue and turquoise. In its center the water disappeared into a circular crater of massive proportions. Joshua was dizzied by the height and the sheer force of the water as it rushed into the abyss below. Behind the two lakes, ice crawled far up the Great Wall reflecting the sunlight in myriads of crystals.

Joshua suddenly knew why it was called the Lake of Tears. It wasn't because of its tear-shaped form. It was because of the spiders mourning their own. He felt a strange connection to them since he knew of their fate. He could no longer be afraid of them. He began to grasp that they were somehow part of the whole that spanned the world around him.

"Joshua," the wolf appeared next to him. "I think I know where we should go. I just don't know how we can find it."

"I had the same thought, Grey."

When they turned they saw Wind and Krieg, dwarfed against the tall window on the other side of the tower.

"Wind, you said the sky people sealed the entrance to the mountain?"

"Yes." Wind answered. "They sealed the entrance. It is completely invisible and cannot be seen. Not by day light, not by moon light, and not in the hours in between. It cannot be found."

As Joshua and Grey walked over the stone floor that was painted in patterns of fading colors, there was the trace of a memory Joshua could not grasp. Whenever he thought he caught it, it eluded him.

"Look around," he thought to them. "Do you see anything out of the ordinary?"

"There is nothing in here, Joshua," Grey answered.

"I know. But there has to be. I can't remember what it is. I'm missing something." Joshua turned, looked through the large windows in all directions; looked beyond them into the landscape and far into the distance.

"Wind, which direction is the sealed entrance you mentioned?" Joshua asked.

"West. The mines are west of here," Wind answered.

Joshua went to the large glass window to the west and looked through it. He concentrated on scanning the Great Wall in the distance for any irregularities.

"Maybe we have to get closer in order to see it," Krieg thought to them.

"Or maybe higher up!" Wind replied "Maybe we have to fly there and see if we can find it from the air"

"It's a possibility. But I don't think that's it," Joshua answered. "Grey, do you remember when we met the large Turtle. It was something she said, I'm sure of it. I just can't remember what it was."

Joshua moved backwards slowly while looking intently through the glass and beyond.

"There is nothing. I can't remember what she said. It's useless. We're never going to find it," Joshua thought more to himself than to the others. At that moment a small beam of sunlight broke through the clouds and for a millisecond, he was blinded by its reflection. Then it was gone.

He looked at his companions.

"I will fly there," Wind thought. "At least it is something I can do. If I can't find it I will come back and see if we can look for it otherwise."

Joshua nodded. "That might be the only way."

"I will go with you," Krieg thought to her.

"You can watch us through the windows. We will return if we don't find anything." Wind, followed by Krieg, was already on her way to the opening in the floor.

"Wait. Wind, wait. I remember… Grey, the turtle said something about glass. A piece of glass. Shattered glass? Do you remember?—"

"The glass is cracked," Grey answered. "She said something about a crack in the glass."

"Yes!" Joshua could not contain his excitement. "A crack in the glass!"

"What does this mean?" Krieg asked.

"I'm not sure. Hold on," he replied, backing away from the westerly window again and this time concentrating on the glass, not on the landscape beyond it. His eyes went up and down, side to side. And when he almost thought it wasn't there, he saw it. It was a small fracture in one of the large glass panels. So small it was completely invisible at first glance.

"Here it is. Look up there!"

Wind and Krieg came back to where Joshua stood. The wolf moved closer as well. They all looked up and now saw a thin and slightly curved horizontal line. The ends were rounded upward.

"Now what?" Grey asked.

"Now we have to find the right angle to look at it," Joshua replied.

"Right angle?" Krieg walked toward the large window. The crack was just above his head.

"Can you see anything?" Joshua asked.

"No," Krieg answered. "Nothing."

"Krieg, may I fly on your back?"

"Sure," Krieg answered.

Joshua flew onto Krieg's back. But he could barely see over the horse's head.

"That's not it either," he thought to the others.

As he looked around he realized that, from up here, the large stone tiles in the floor didn't look that random anymore. There was a symmetry to it that he did not recognize before.

"Krieg, I have an idea but it seems foolish even as I think it," Joshua thought.

"What is it?" Krieg answered.

Joshua looked up to the ceiling high above them. The thought alone made him squirm.

"Can you take me up there?"

Krieg looked up. About eight stories above them the walls met the half round dome like ceiling.

"Are you sure you want me to?" Krieg asked.

"Yes. No. Yes." Joshua suddenly wasn't so sure anymore. It more and more felt like a silly idea. He could sense Grey's concern for Krieg.

"Forget it I… it doesn't make sense. Forget it," Joshua thought.

"I'll take you," Krieg answered.

Joshua looked at Krieg. So did Wind. She nodded ever so slightly. Grey gave his silent approval as well and stepped back to give Krieg the space he needed.

"Be careful," Wind's thoughts whispered. "You don't have a hundred yards."

"I will be," he answered.

And with that, he unfolded his wings and moved backwards toward the corner. He figured he had about fourty yards to take off. Not enough.

"Krieg, are you sure you can do this?" Joshua asked, feeling his apprehension.

"Yes. I can do this for you. For us. Just hold on tight."

He went on his hind legs and jumped forward. Joshua dug his talons into Krieg's coat and tried to stay as low as possible as they gained speed and power. The other side of the large room came closer fast. Krieg's massive wings pushed downward, creating an upward draft and suddenly they were in the air. Too close to the other corner, Krieg wasn't able to turn. He had to use all his strength to push upward and not stall and fall like a stone. Slowly—too slow for Joshua—they gained height and moved away from the corner toward the middle of the room. Joshua felt a wave of dizziness washing over him as he looked down. From up here Wind and Grey seemed small in comparison to the large dome. He looked from them onto the floor.

And suddenly he saw it. Krieg must have seen it at the same time. A frightened gasp escaped the horse and for a moment Joshua thought he would lose control. But Krieg caught himself and for a few seconds they hovered high above looking down into the face of a lioness.

Her face was painted into the mosaic of the floor tiles, impossible to see from below. But from up here her head filled the entire floor. Her green eyes seemed to penetrate deep into Joshua's soul. There were white markings on her cheeks, a pink nose and dark patches between her eyes and on her forehead. There was no danger in her expression. Just clear and unchallenged authority. Joshua heard her thoughts echoing inside his mind.

"If you want to continue on this journey you must find me deep within you. Otherwise the mountain will not release you once you have entered its domain."

Her thoughts stirred something inside Joshua, something he could not yet grasp or even begin to understand. For a few moments longer they hovered high above. Joshua could not look away from her. She held his gaze until they landed next to their companions. From here the face of the lioness had once again disappeared. There were only pieces of colored stone with no unified pattern at all. Her thoughts, however, stood clear in Joshua's mind, her image unmistakably connected to them. It became clear to him at that moment that what she had told him were not mere suggestions. She had given him an order that he would do well to heed.

* * *

Wind was the first to break the silence that held them all within its spell. She began to weep quietly.

"You have seen the lioness, Joshua," she thought to him.

"Yes, I have." Still stunned by what he had witnessed, Joshua looked from Wind to Grey.

"We have seen her through your eyes," the wolf answered his gaze. "Until this moment I thought her a mere legend, no more than myth carried through the generations. But when I saw her it was as if I knew her and have known her since the dawn of time."

"This changes everything," Wind thought to them.

"What do you mean?" Joshua asked.

"I am not sure. What I do know is that no one can look upon the lioness and be the same again."

Everyone stood quietly for a while following the trail of their own thoughts. Wind walked toward the middle of the room.

"I know what you must do" her thoughts reached them. "Look down here."

Joshua flew down from Krieg's back and walked toward Wind.

"I saw it through your eyes. You might not remember. Your glimpse of her was too short. But look right here. Between her eyes."

Where she stood, Joshua saw that two of the stone tiles were cracked. The shape of it was similar to the crack in the glass.

"You must stand here and look beyond the glass. But not only you. The three of you. The three of you came here. The three of you must find your way deep into the mountain."

Joshua understood. So did Grey and Krieg. The horse walked over to stand with his front legs just before the crack.

"Can you make it up here, Grey?" Krieg asked.

"I think so," the wolf answered.

"Do it." Krieg stood, bracing himself while Grey trotted back ten yards and then turned and charged toward the horse. Just before Joshua thought he would crash into him, the wolf jumped and landed on Krieg's back.

"Now it's your turn," Krieg thought to Joshua. "Come up here, red one, and tell us what you see."

Joshua flew up and landed on the wolf's back. In front of Joshua, about 15 yards away, was the west facing window with the crack just below his eye level. Beyond it in the distance the Great Wall extended upward into the sky. Joshua let his gaze rest on the small fracture and then go beyond it. Nothing happened. He tried to switch his focal point between the crack in the glass and the wall in the distance. Nothing.

"I can't see anything," he thought.

"Wait, Joshua." Wind's thoughts came to him like a whisper, a quiet breeze over fields of deepest green. "Wait and be still."

And when Joshua forgot for one moment whether he should concentrate on the crack or the wall beyond, when he just let his eyes rest on nothing in particular, a shape suddenly carved itself out of the Great Wall. It was almost as if it sprang toward him. The three dimensional outline reminded him of the head of the lioness he had seen just before. But where the other was still, more detailed and directed inward, this one looked as if it was jumping straight at him. Joshua flew up in terror letting out a crow that echoed through the large dome. Grey jumped off the horse and Krieg went on his hind legs. For a moment the terror went through each of them like a wave crashing against the rocks.

"What was that?" Grey fought his instinct to run in the opposite direction.

"I don't have the slightest idea," Krieg answered. "But whatever it was, I don't think it wants us to come anywhere near it."

When Joshua looked toward the Wall it was normal again. There was no indication where the head of the lioness had just been.

"I know where we have to go," Joshua sounded much more certain than he was.

"Where?" Grey asked.

"Do you see the small body of water straight ahead, right at the bottom of the wall?" Joshua looked in the direction of it.

"I can see it," Wind thought to them.

"That's where we have to go. That's where we will find the entrance and the Porte Des Lioness.

Dwarfed against the large window and looking out over the wide landscape below, the four companions stood next to each other in the sun flooded hall. It dawned on Joshua that, as far as they had come and whatever their journey had been up until now, it was only just the beginning.

14. Darkness

D eep inside the Ice Forest, high up in a tree, under the dark covers of the night she woke. Her cold dead eyes scanned the darkness around her. Her partially decomposed, disease riddled body held the stench of death and decay. Just before she woke, she had a dream of a large cave and of three feathers that lay on a blackened stone deep inside a mountain. In her dream she saw the rooster and she knew that she could not let him find what he was looking for. Something stirred deep within her and whatever it was it brought her back to the living enough to escape death for a while longer.

"Feed on the dead," the darkness whispered. "And make me an army worthy of what I am."

She pushed off the branch, circling the air. Her massive wings easily spanned twelve yards; her talons could hold a grown wolf in them and carry him up into the air so she could feed on him in mid flight. The Griffon Vulture set course toward Hollow's Gate. She flew fast, close to the tip of the trees and her cries were heard far into the forest and every beast was reminded how close it was to death, how easily its little life could be snapped from it.

She flew for ten days and ten nights and at dawn of the eleventh day she reached Hollow's Gate from the south east. From high above she saw the rooster and the wolf fall into the deep. She watched the war horse and the Pegasus escape from the crumbling path and witnessed the sky people floating up within the light beam. Her eyes blinded by it, she withdrew and watched the Pegasus and the horse from high up in a tree. And when the war horse jumped off the cliff, she followed him. As he disappeared into the Gate of Time, she hovered there and within the darkness of Time's Gate where past and future were there with her, she clearly saw the end of the Rooster in her mind. She saw the Pegasus as she hung held by hundreds of thin threads above a black abyss; she saw the wolf fight for the rooster's life and she saw the war horse fall from high above, inside the mountain, paralyzed by the deep festering cuts of her talons and wounds from her beak. She saw it all and knew the certain outcome of her task. And she was content.

When she flew out of the blackness, gliding through the air high above Hollow's Gate, she heard the eagle's cry close to the Wall. Ayres, the Guardian of the Gate came toward her. His speed could match hers. His size could not. She killed him instantly, her beak feeding on his flesh before she dropped his remains into the deep. She landed eventually at the bottom of the waterfall, close to where Joshua and the Wolf had been only a few days past. The hyenas, six of them, were in different stages of decomposition, a foul stench of decay lay over them like a blanket. She resurrected them all, not to what they had been before but to something else—creatures of darkness, starved, poised to attack, shrieking in wrath and allowed to feed only on what they would bring back to her, their master.

The hyenas and the vulture went around the city of ruins unable to penetrate the light shield. They felt the cold claws of the ice reach for them from deep underground when they made their way toward the Refuge. But the ice had no power over them for it could only take from the living and not from the dead. When the spiders died on their way to the Refuge, the vulture brought them all back. She brought them back to serve one purpose: To hunt down the rooster, to capture the Pegasus and to kill and feed on the wolf and the war horse. Such was their purpose now. The hundreds and hundreds of spiders the ice had left to die followed their master into the holes inside the earth from whence they came.

When the ice withdrew, the remaining spiders searched for their kin, unable to grasp what had happened. They went back the way they came, up the small path through the trees and egg shaped boulders and into their holes that would lead them deep underground and to their home. They never reached it. Their brethren, no longer recognizing their own kin, killed them and they joined the ranks of the army of the dark. And then they waited.

15. Alda

When the four companions made their way down the massive staircase of the Refuge, Joshua thought about what they would encounter outside the tower. He still held the gruesome image of the spider's bodies in his mind as they lay scattered, some floating in the lake, others on the path across it. But as they stepped into the sunlight and onto the small platform, there was no trace of them anywhere. The surviving spiders had probably taken care of their own, carrying them back deep underground according to their custom.

They crossed the narrow walkway from the Refuge to the shore. With the ice gone, Joshua could see far down into the deep blue, crystal clear lake. He remembered Alda telling them that it had no bottom and the thought of it made him shiver.

"Do you hear that?" Wind who was ahead of him on the walkway stopped.

"What is it?" Krieg asked.

"It's a melody," she replied.

"It's coming from the lake," Krieg stopped as well.

Now Joshua could hear it too.

"I know this. I have known this…" Wind turned toward the lake. "I have known this melody since I was still a foal. How can this be? I don't understand—"

"TURTLE!" The wolf's thought reached them at the same time as, about fifty yards out, the massive turtle broke through the surface of the water like a huge wale. Her jump was accompanied by a crescendo of the melody she created. At the moment the melody stopped, she crashed back into the water, the impact creating a tidal wave that rushed toward the walkway with immense speed. Grey ran the remaining distance to the shore and just made it before the wave washed over the walkway. Joshua jumped up and avoided being taken by it. Krieg and the horse didn't move but the water wasn't high enough to have an impact on them.

"My friends!" The turtle's thoughts were loud as thunder as she swam toward the shore. "Sorry, I didn't mean to be so loud but I am very excited to see you again. There is the wolf and my red friend. I see that you made it safely to the Refuge. I hope my thoughts about the spiders reached you. I just wanted to let you know not to be afraid of them and that they would not harm you."

The turtle was just about to reach the shore when she saw Wind. She stopped her movement and floated in the water only a few yards from the walkway.

"Is that you?" Her thoughts were but a whisper now. "Wind, is that you?"

"Alda? I thought my eyes betrayed me when I first saw you." The joy spilled out from Wind and onto the others. She went on her hind legs, her wings spreading wide as the turtle moved her massive head forward and toward her.

"Alda," their heads were now close together and Wind rubbed her nose on the turtle's. "I'm so glad to see you again!"

"The last thing I heard was that you went to the surface and into the Ice Forest. That was...that must have been after the beacon had been destroyed."

For an instant Joshua thought he saw shame in Wind's eyes. As if whatever had happened was connected to some wrong doing on her part. But a moment later her lightness came back.

"I have missed you. But what are you doing here and how do you know my friends?"

"How much time do you have?" Alda waved her head slowly from one side to the other.

Joshua heard a soft melody in the background. It reminded him of something that he couldn't quite pinpoint.

"I have known Wind from when she was a foal," the turtle's thoughts sang out to them. "There were at least a dozen foals in my care at any given time. Wind was one of the brightest. I was there the day she got her wings."

"Alda, this is Krieg. It was he, together with Grey, the wolf and Joshua, the rooster, who freed me from the stone."

"I did not know you were captured there and I was not aware of a way that once you turn to stone you can be brought back," the Turtle's head turned toward the horse.

"It looks to me that your friends have been true to you from the beginning. Krieg, I do not remember you as a foal and I don't think any of the other Pegasus were left alive. It seems that you have fought a different kind of battle in a different place and time. It takes years of preparation for a horse to learn to fly. Whatever you did in the past must have prepared you for it somehow. One never knows when one is ready to break through, to reach beyond the little self and to cross the threshold into a bigger world."

At the last words Alda had turned her head toward Joshua. "Where we came from does not matter," she continued. "Whatever our confines have been in the past they have no meaning now other than what our own belief bestows upon them."

Joshua felt her thoughts resonating in his mind even though they made him uncomfortable.

"There are no limits to what you can do, my small but mighty friend. Remember this when doubt seems to cloud your mind. You can reach far beyond yourself. You can and you must. For there is more that hangs in the balance here than you and I can see. I can feel it in the deep, far down at the place where all the water in Hollow's Gate is connected. I will return there in due time. But for now, who's up for a ride on the lake?"

They glanced at each other. The thought of standing on the turtle's shell and swimming over an abyss of infinite depth made Joshua's skin crawl.

"I don't... know," he thought.

Krieg moved slightly backwards as well. It was Grey who jumped onto the turtle's massive back first. He was followed by Wind.

"Come," she thought to Krieg. "You will not forget this."

Krieg thought about it only for a moment before he jumped onto the turtle's back.

"Come on, Joshua, there is still plenty of space. I once carried thirteen foals across the lake and I was only half the size I am now."

Joshua looked at his companions. He didn't realize until now that he hadn't considered Wind to be one of them. Looking at her standing next to Krieg, he felt the depth of her connection to the war horse and Krieg's growing fondness of her. But he also felt their inclusion of himself into their bond and he felt Grey's undying loyalty to him and his strong sense of protection toward him and the others. And somehow in jumping onto the back of the turtle they all agreed to welcome Alda into their circle of friendship as well.

Joshua flew up and onto the massive shell. The moment he landed, Alda pushed away from the shore and swam a few strokes backwards. Joshua crouched down for fear of losing his balance. The surface of the shell was rough with petrified growths dating back centuries. For an instant Joshua grasped how old Alda must be, how many lifetimes she must have walked this earth and swam the lakes.

"You must know these lands well," Joshua thought.

"I do. I did," the turtle answered while turning and pushing away from the shore and into the open water. "Slowly but surely it all comes back to me. Still much is in the dark but I can see glimpses here and there and those are enough to help me remember. There was a time when everything seemed to be in balance. When the sky people and the Pegasus lived in peace together at Hollow's Gate. That was the time where my memories are the most vivid. But when the mines were opened and it became known that this place held treasures no one could even imagine, the balance shifted and it triggered an avalanche that, once in motion, could not be stopped. The pendulum reached its tipping point and stopped. The beacon was destroyed. The Pegasus that weren't killed fled Hollow's Gate. And times grew dark once more."

As Joshua listened to Alda's story and followed her trail of thought he felt the breeze in his feathers and the mist of the gushing water in his face. From here Refuge looked even more majestic than from inland. It towered high above them, its glass top reflecting the sun light and the clouds in the sky. From Joshua's point of view, in the middle of the large lake was what looked like an indentation in its surface. He remembered from back in the tower that the water disappeared there into a large round opening, like a funnel. Joshua suddenly felt uneasy, as if sensing an invisible pull toward the center of the lake and one that could not be escaped.

"Do not be afraid, Joshua," the turtle reassured him. "The gravitational pull is minimal. As you might have noticed, the natural laws of Hollow's Gate are different from the ones on the surface. I will not let any harm come to you."

Joshua didn't see any reason not to trust Alda. However, there was a small part of him that wasn't certain, that still thought it needed to stay alert and ready.

"Alda, I would like to go back into the city," Wind's thoughts brushed against Joshua's mind. "I have many questions and I wish so much to stand inside the great city of light once more."

"I will accompany you," Alda answered. "We shall go there together. I'm sure our three friends here have to continue on their own journey."

"We have to find the entrance to the mountain, the Porte Des Lioness," Joshua replied. "I was hoping you could come with us and help us find it."

"If you need help, you will find it there, my feathered friend. For now, I shall accompany Wind into the city. It will help us both remember more of our past."

Wind stood close to Krieg, her forehead touching his neck. "You could come with us. It would be a great joy to show you the place I was born in, where I grew up."

"I would love nothing more," Krieg replied. "But I promised my little rooster friend to try to help him find what he is looking for and I think I should keep true to that promise."

"I understand. And we shall meet you at the entrance to the mountain afterwards. For I wish to help him as well."

They rode quietly for a while, each of them lost in their own thoughts. Wind thought about the places of her childhood and some of the memories that, so long buried deep within her mind, began to creep up into consciousness. They were only images, incomplete at best but nevertheless part of a whole that, given time, would all come to the surface. But some of those memories were not filled with light and laughter and a carefree childhood. There were darker ones pushed even further down that rose with the others. It would take a while for her to allow them all to arise and then sort through them. She was certain that going back into the city would help her with that.

"You have been quiet of late, Grey," Joshua looked at the wolf who lay across from him. "Is there anything that keeps your thoughts occupied?"

Grey held his gaze for a moment. "Since I have seen the face of the lioness up at the tower, something has changed."

"It has to do with your companion?" Joshua asked.

"I believe so. Since I saw the lioness I have had the sense that the memories of my companion have moved closer, her presence stronger in my thoughts. What I saw in the lioness reminded me of her and it brought her closer to me. At the same time it seems to hurt more. As if an old wound that was about to heal had been pried open and exposed to the elements once again. I feel at once better than I have for a long time and also much worse. In telling you this I realize how little I am making sense right now."

The wolf looked away from Joshua and toward the tower of Refuge.

"I have also been thinking for a while now that whatever it is that awaits us inside the mountain, is probably not what we expect it to be. There might be answers there but I also know that they might not come in ways that we will understand or even want to. I cannot shake the uneasy feeling I get when my thoughts go there. Part of me thinks we should stay away from it. Far away."

"I know what you speak of, Grey. I have been feeling it myself. And if you tell me now that you think it better not to go I will obey your wishes. We can stay here or somehow find our way back to the surface."

"We might not even find the entrance to the mountain. It has been sealed centuries ago and I'm sure whoever did it, thought to not let anyone that just came along cross the threshold. I think the entrance might be harder to find than we think."

As Joshua thought of this, he realized that the turtle had slowed down and was almost at a complete stop, floating in the water.

"Why are we stopping?" Joshua asked.

There was no answer for a while.

"Do you trust me, Joshua?" He heard the turtle's thoughts.

"Yes," he answered without even thinking about it. "Yes I do."

"I'm so sorry I have to do this to you but I just remembered something."

With that, the turtle suddenly dropped down and her whole body disappeared into the water. Joshua didn't have time to react. In an instant, he found himself half under the surface desperately gasping for air. He sank like a stone. In looking up he saw the silhouettes of the wolf and the two horses above him. He saw Grey try to reach him under water but he couldn't get to him. Below him was the blackness of the abyss and in a moment of terror, Joshua realized that he was going to die and that there was nothing anybody could do about it. The question 'why?' briefly crossed his mind but before he could follow that thought he suddenly saw Alda in front of him. She was facing him under water.

"Joshua, swim to the surface!" Her thoughts told him.

"I can't! I can't swim."

"You can, Joshua."

"I can't! Help me!"

"I am helping you. Now swim to the surface!"

"I'm can't swim underwater. You have to help me or I'll drown."

The panic he felt was overwhelming. He realized that he was getting weaker. He would have to do something really soon if he didn't want to drown. He tried desperately to use his talons but it didn't do much at all.

"Push yourself up." The turtle's thoughts got louder in his mind.

"I can't!"

"Push yourself up!"

"I CAN'T! DON'T YOU UNDERSTAND! I'M NOT MADE TO SWIM UNDER WATER!"

More out of frustration, he pushed his wings downward gaining an upward lift.

"Do it again, Joshua!" The turtle's face was right in front of him. Why didn't she just help him up?

"DO IT AGAIN, JOSHUA!" Her thoughts were a crescendo, a cacophony of sound. More than anything he wanted to escape THAT. He pushed upward again. And again. He saw the light coming closer but he also felt that he didn't have much more left in him.

"Only a few more, Joshua!" Alda's thoughts left no room for anything else in his mind.

"Push!" He thought to himself.

"Push downward to go upward!" The turtle thought to him.

"Push downward to go upward!" He repeated her thought while squeezing the last ounce of strength out of his tired wings.

And then he broke through the surface of the lake taking in a deep breath of air. It took a few moments before he could orient himself. He saw Grey, Krieg and Wind swimming close together not far away.

"Are you alright?" Wind asked.

Before he could say anything he saw that the three of them were lifted up and out of the water.

"I'm so sorry. Hold on, coming up!" The turtle's thoughts were loud but not unbearable.

Suddenly Joshua felt the turtle's shell under his talons as she came out of the water.

"I'm so very sorry I had to do this to you."

Grey shook himself. Wind and Krieg unfolded their wings moving them up and down several times to get at least some of the water out of them.

"Alda what was that?" Wind thought.

"I'm so sorry," the turtle replied. "I'm so very sorry. I remembered something and I thought it was very important at the time that I did what I did but now I can't remember anymore and it feels so silly and I'm so sorry to have done this to you."

Her words were accompanied by a frantic melody that didn't seem to have any rhyme or reason to it.

"Alda!" Wind moved toward her head and looked down at her. "Alda, can you please stop the music."

"Oh. Yes. So sorry!"

And suddenly it was quiet. Joshua didn't realize how loud and frantic the melody was until it was gone. He got up and shook himself several times, still in shock over what had just happened. He could have easily drowned.

"Joshua." He heard Alda in his thoughts, quiet now and not more than a whisper. "You must know that even though I cannot remember why I did what I did, I would have never let you drown. Never."

Joshua wasn't sure what to think at that moment. "Next time a little warning would be good," he replied.

"Where you are going, my dear friend, there will be no warning." Alda's thoughts were quiet. A simple statement. Its power resonated within him. A sense of foreboding crept up in Joshua that he could neither deny nor push away. He realized that inevitably they would reach a point where they could not turn back any longer, where they could only go forward. He dreaded that moment already, knowing that it would come eventually.

Krieg came over and gave him a slight nudge with his nose. "Are you okay?" He asked.

"Yes, I will be. I guess. Once all the liquid has drained out of my nostrils and lungs," Joshua replied. Krieg smiled in his thoughts.

And that was that. Alda brought them safely back to shore where they jumped off her large back and onto the rocky shore that surrounded the lake. When the turtle came out of the water under many apologies for the rushing stream that came out of every crevice of her shell, Joshua was reminded again how big she was. Her head and neck alone were easily as long as Krieg. It would take her and Wind a while to reach the city, and even longer to get back to them. He just hoped he would find the entrance somehow and that he wouldn't have made this journey for nothing.

"Joshua," Alda's thought interrupted his.

"Yes," he answered.

"For naught is nothing that you do, my dear friend. You will find the entrance into the mountain and you will find what you are looking for. I will see you again soon, I hope," her large eyes looked at him and he could see the kindness in them and her well wishes for his journey. Krieg said his good bye's to Wind and the three of them watched the Pegasus and Alda as they slowly walked through the valley and toward the path that led through the egg shaped boulders and spider trees up the hill that would eventually lead into the city of light ruins.

For a while they could hear the turtle's humming until it faded from their thoughts. Joshua couldn't help but feel a sense of finality in their parting. He brushed the thought away and concentrated on the path ahead. It lead through the hills in the opposite direction along the rocky shore of the lake. The Refuge became smaller and smaller the longer they walked. Krieg looked back once in a while until Wind and Alda disappeared behind a hill. Joshua could sense his friend's pain over parting with her. He jumped onto the horses' back.

"You will see her again," Joshua thought to him. "You will see her again soon." And if he had doubted this before, he had forgotten all about it by now.

The Great Wall rose before them, still a day's walk away but within reach. Joshua thought of the next part of their journey and of what would await them. If he had known what was in store for them, he would have turned around and he would have fled and nothing and no one would have been able to stop him.

16. Capture

They traveled west along the river that fed the Lake of Tears. To the south the glacier reached almost to its shore. The ice spanned from here to the southern part of the wall and a quarter of the way up, like hands reaching to the heavens. The ice of the glacier had a green hue to it as if it had come on suddenly, instantly freezing plants, grasses and vegetation, and from then on holding them in its cold embrace. The sun was at their back, illuminating the wall ahead in tones of gold and shimmering earth colors. Joshua figured that they didn't have more than a day and a half of sunlight left before darkness would settle once more in Hollow's Gate. They needed to reach the Porte Des Lioness by then for without the light of the beacon they had no protection from whatever creatures the night released upon them.

Joshua was still not convinced that they would be able to find the actual entrance. He had seen the contours of the head of the lioness embedded in the wall for only a brief moment. That glimpse had been too brief to remember any specific details now. The only part that had stayed with him was the small body of water he had seen right below it. If they followed the river there was a good chance that they would find the entrance.

From here, the wall looked flat, smooth and impenetrable. Nothing gave even the slightest indication of the head of the lioness. Joshua became more and more convinced that whatever he had seen from high up in the tower was an optical illusion, some kind of device to induce enough fear in whoever looked at it to stay far away. But something didn't quite make sense here. Why go through all the trouble to make whoever searches for it stand exactly at a certain spot and look through the cracked glass at exactly the right location to then be told to not go any further? Was it a warning, meant for the few who figured out where to look not to enter?

The more he thought about it the more it felt to Joshua that he was part of a game someone else played and just a figure in it and nothing more. But that was exactly the opposite of what he had felt when he saw the head of the lioness in the tiles of the tower room. He felt her strength and her unchallenged authority and even though he could not feel her within himself she had told him, in no uncertain terms, that it was crucial for him to look for her and find her. Was that the answer? What did he know that he didn't realize he knew? What was in him that lay idle and unnoticed under thick layers of fear and his belief that he couldn't possibly be part of something larger than himself? But wasn't that what he had set out to finding in the first place? What did he fly out of the pen for, other than to find something that was greater than himself? But would he find it deep inside a mountain?

They had crossed the crest of a small hill. From here the path along the river in front of them lead all the way to where the river ended in a small pond at the bottom of the Great Wall. The pond itself lay in the shadows as the sun was setting behind the rim of Hollow's Gate. Night would come soon. If they wouldn't be able to find the entrance in daylight, what were the chances of finding it at night? And who knew what would be waiting for them down here once the sun had set completely.

For a while now, Joshua had felt the presence of his companions next to him. He realized that it wasn't necessary to form a specific thought and communicate it with them in order for him to feel their bond. They had been walking for hours with very little conversation between them. However, he could sense Grey's and Krieg's presence without words now and he knew they had shared in his thoughts and ideas along the way. He knew of Krieg's thoughts about Wind and the sting of her absence in his heart. Here and there her thoughts brushed against Krieg's mind, and Joshua glimpsed an image of her and Alda as they began their slow ascent on the path up the hill that would eventually lead them past the entrances to the spider holes and into the city of light ruins.

"I should have gone with her," Krieg interrupted Joshua's thoughts. "I shouldn't have let her go alone."

"She can take care of herself, Krieg," Grey replied. "And she is not alone. They should easily reach the city during daylight."

"I think we made a mistake," Krieg's thoughts were accompanied by a sudden sense of fear. "If they reach the city just before dark they will have to stay there for a week in order to be safe. In order for us to make it, we have to be inside the mountain by then."

"She can fly back, Krieg," Joshua tried to sound more convinced than he was. "It would only be a short distance through the air. And Alda has survived many nights down here."

Krieg thought about this. "I guess you're right," he replied.

Joshua could sense Krieg's conflict of whether or not he should stay with them or go to find Wind and go with her. Joshua looked at Grey who gave his silent approval.

"Krieg, if you wish to go and make sure she is ok we can meet you both at the entrance. It will take us a while to find it anyway," Joshua thought.

"If you don't mind, I would like to go to see her safely reach the city."

"Go," Grey answered. "We will search for the entrance and meet you both there."

Joshua flew down from the horse's back to stand in front of him. Krieg bowed his head and gently touched Joshua's head with his nose.

"Go," Joshua thought quietly to him. "We will wait for your return."

Krieg exchanged a short glance with Grey, then turned around and first trotted, then began to gallop. When his wings unfolded he lifted up and with powerful flaps he rose into the air.

* * *

Wind and Alda had reached the area of the egg-shaped boulders and made their way up the windy path. In her conversation with the turtle, Wind had discovered memories that she thought she had lost. They were memories of her childhood when she was raised in a group of foals. Each foal was given to the care of one of the children of the sky people. The sky children made sure that each foal had enough food and water; they brushed them and took them out to ride regularly. The child Wind was given to was called Leannah. But it wasn't only Leannah that took care of the foal. The connection and responsibility was mutual and reciprocal. Child and foal taught each other of each other and so began to form a bond that would last a life time.

When Alda told her the story of Leannah, Wind was overcome with emotion, surprised over the strength of the bond she still felt to the child. She did not remember what had become of her. Only that, one day, shortly after Wind had gotten her wings, the children were taken and brought deep underground to work in the mines. The day the men came to take Leannah out of the stables was so clear and vivid, it seemed to Wind as if it had happened yesterday. But she also felt that there was still an area of her memory that was clouded in mist and inaccessible to both her and Alda. It was a memory of a darker time, a time that forgetfulness still kept in its merciful embrace.

Wind was glad for Alda's lighter memories and Alda was happy to share them with her, as they were her memories as well. So deeply were they immersed in their conversation, that Wind thought she had stumbled over a root or part of a branch at first. But when it happened to her other foot she looked down and saw a bundle of white threads, sticky and thick, wrapped around her ankles.

"What is this?" She thought to Alda who walked slightly ahead of her. The turtle turned her head. Her eyes widened and Wind instinctively opened her wings. But before she could unfold them they were covered in more of the sticky threads. At the same time, both her front legs were pulled from under her and she fell down.

Now she could see behind her. There were hundreds and hundreds of spiders moving toward them. Out of her peripheral vision she saw many more spilling out of the holes in the ground.

"I thought they weren't dangerous," was the last clear thought Wind could form. To the crescendo of Alda's cacophonous music, and within moments, the spiders had wrapped Wind in a cocoon from which there was no escape. She fought it but that tightened the spider's web and made it more impenetrable. Alda saw terror in Wind's eyes when she was taken; first pulled then carried by countless spiders up toward one of the holes.

The turtle turned. Too slowly she moved her massive body under enormous strain as fast as she could toward the hole into which the Pegasus had been carried. Most of the spiders had disappeared already. They left as fast as they came, lead by one single terror-inducing command. When moments later the turtle was alone, she heard the cries of the Griffon Vulture as she landed less than five yards from Alda's head. The vulture brought with her the stench of death and decay and the insane. Her feathers were blackened, half decomposed. A slimy liquid dripped out of her mouth. One eye was grey, blind yet looking at her from beyond, demanding her attention.

"I should have remembered," Alda thought to herself. "I could have remembered."

"Yes. You could have saved them all. Too late now. A pity." The Vulture cocked her head. "All the wisdom of the world is at your disposal and you forgot? Remember this: I will wait for the dreamer, the red rooster, inside the mountain. If he does not come, the Pegasus dies. And I will make sure to take my time with her. The last thing I will feast on is her heart and she will die knowing that she has failed to fulfill her destiny."

The moment the vulture spread her massive wings to fly off, Alda saw a shadow blocking the low sun for a moment. She saw the silhouette of the war horse coming toward them from above. The vulture saw him also. Krieg landed and galloped the last part of the distance between himself and the vulture. When he reached her, the vulture lifted off and with only a few powerful flaps of her wings was already high up in the air, her eerie cries hollow and poised to fester in Krieg's mind telling him of his own demise. Krieg turned around and galloped in long strides then lifted off gaining height and momentum. He turned in the air to face her. The vulture flew toward him, wings wide, talons spread, her blind eye fixed on the war horse. Krieg had fought many battles; most of them head on toward the enemy. He did not withdraw from her.

They met in mid air high above the ground and even though Krieg was bigger and his anger fueled by the pain of what happened to Wind, he had no chance against the vulture. She ripped her talons into the side of his neck and down toward his belly. The only thing that saved him were his powerful hind legs. He hit her once and pushed her away from him.

"You cannot defeat me in the air, war horse!" Her thoughts screamed at him. "This is my home. Up here you are nothing!"

Krieg had trouble staying in the air, his right wing suddenly flooded with pain. He sank fast barely making it to the ground without crashing. When he landed next to Alda, the vulture flew low over their heads, her cries penetrating deep into their souls.

"You will die and in death you will feed me and my army and make us more powerful than we have ever been before. Darkness will take you and never let you go. You will stay in its icy claws until your life gives way to death and then you will belong to me forever!" The vulture made one final low swoop and disappeared from their sight. Krieg stood panting, blood dripping from his side.

"Krieg I'm so sorry, I should have remembered. I could have warned you and the others. It comes in bits and pieces and fades again soon thereafter. There was something about the dreamer of light and that…by his very dreaming, he somehow awakens his dark counterpart… But this is my fault. I lead Wind straight to her. How could I have missed this? How could I have forgotten this?"

"There was nothing you could have done," Krieg thought to her. "We just have to find the entrance to the mountain and somehow get her back."

"Go, fly to your friends. I can't make it into the mountain. No entrance will be big enough for me."

"I shouldn't leave you here—"

"You must go, Krieg! I have lived here for a thousand years. I know how to defend myself. But you must go and bring her back. Do you hear me? Bring her back to me!"

"I shall."

Alda's and Krieg's forehead touched for a brief moment. Then Krieg turned and galloped over the meadow until he had enough speed to take flight. Aware of the waves of pain in his side and his right wing, Krieg pushed through it and despite it gained height and speed.

"Bring her back..." the turtle's thoughts trailed off until they were gone. It was an hour's flight from here to Joshua's and the Grey's last position. Krieg just hoped he would not encounter the vulture on his way there for he would not be able to fight her again today.

17. Broga

hen Joshua saw it, he stopped and turned around. It was, at first only a dot in the landscape but it came closer fast.

"What is this?" Grey asked and stopped as well.

They had made good progress and were about three quarters of the way between the Lake of Tears and the pond below the Great Wall. Grey had discovered a narrow path that did not follow the river but cut a relatively straight line toward the pond. They had stopped only once and only for Grey to catch a few muskrats by the river and for Joshua to find some berries. They had been starving. Joshua thought that if they could maintain their current speed, they would have about half a day of walking left until they reached the water. From there it was just a matter of figuring out how to find the entrance. He didn't have any illusions about how hard it would be. It was put in place by the sky people who didn't want anyone to gain access to the mountain. Another thought that kept coming back to him was that the entrance may have simply collapsed over time and because of it, there was no way into the mountain at all anymore.

"It's Krieg!" Grey saw him first. The war horse ran in full gallop toward them, pulling a dust cloud behind him. Before he caught up to them, they could hear his panic stricken thoughts. "Wind. Taken.

Spiders," were the only fragments Joshua could decipher, so erratic were the horse's thoughts.

"They took her," Krieg's thoughts poured out of him when he arrived and his emotions hit Joshua and Grey like a battering ram. "They took her into the mountain. I came too late. They captured her."

"Who captured her?" The wolf asked.

"Spiders. And a Griffon Vulture," Krieg replied.

"Spiders?" Joshua was surprised. "I thought they were harmless."

"They were," Krieg answered. "They were harmless until the vulture resurrected the dead ones. She said she will wait inside the mountain for us. She wants to exchange Wind for you, Joshua."

They looked at each other. Krieg's right wing was lifted up showing the deep blood filled and infested markings the vulture had left. Joshua could sense Krieg's pain.

"You fought her?" Grey asked.

"Yes," Krieg answered. "I had no chance against her in the air. Alda mentioned something about a dark counterpart to the dreamer of light. I think she meant you, Joshua."

"Me?" Joshua was surprised. "I don't understand."

"The eagle has told me about her," Grey thought.

"What? Why didn't you tell me?" Joshua asked.

"I didn't want to upset you," the wolf answered. "Also, I thought it a myth, not a reality."

"A myth? What kind of myth?"

"The eagle spoke about a dark counterpart to the dreamer of light who was awakened the same time as the dreamer."

"A counterpart?" Joshua had trouble grasping the idea and its full implications.

"Yes. The dreamer who sets out to find the three feathers inevitably awakens the dark counter part of himself. If you are on one tipping point of the pendulum, Joshua, the Griffon Vulture is on the other side. She is the darkness to your light. She is your opposite."

Joshua thought about this. Why hadn't he heard of this before? There were other legends he had known of or heard of in the past. Not this one.

"Krieg, I'm so sorry about Wind."

"We have to find her and get her back," Krieg answered. "I cannot bear to think about her being captured like this when she had just escaped her prison a few days past. The time of freedom that was given her was too short. Far too short… We have to find her and free her."

"We will, Krieg. I promise you," Joshua was surprised at the strength this thought evoked in him. He felt fear, yes, but he also felt something else deep inside him that stirred, that moved, small still but there nevertheless. It was the image of the lioness that brought forth this response in him.

"We will find her, Krieg. And when we do, we will save her."

"Then let us go and find the entrance to the mountain and let us be swift," the wolf answered. "Krieg, can you fly?" Joshua thought.

"I don't think so. The claws of the vulture must have severed a muscle or at least injured it in such a way that I can't use this wing for long. But I can run, Joshua. Come on my back."

Before Krieg could finish the thought, Joshua had already jumped up and the horse began to trot. Grey ran in front of them and both found a speed that they could sustain for a while. Joshua could almost physically feel Krieg's pain. The cuts were deep and infested and each step caused his wing to brush against them. But the pain in the horse's body was nothing compared to the pain he felt for Wind in his heart. Joshua knew that the mighty war horse had at last found an enemy that he did not wish to meet in battle: the notion that he had lost Wind and that she would not survive.

They ran the remainder of the distance without stopping for water or rest. Joshua still had no idea how to get inside the mountain. And another question rose inside him. It was the question as to how the vulture would get Wind into the mountain. If the entrance was sealed and if the Porte Des Lioness was the only way in… But maybe there was another entrance and one they could also find. Joshua kept looking ahead toward the pond that was now clearly visible in the distance. There was nothing but the sheer cliff of the Great Wall above it, with no sign of an entrance whatsoever. Until he saw it.

Just like up in the tower room when he saw the head of the lioness jump out at him, it suddenly became visible. And because the path they took lead straight toward it, it was hidden to them up until now. Joshua realized that they did not go toward the head of the lioness. They were about to go into its mouth. They were walking towards a massive outcropping of rock that jutted straight out of the wall and was shaped like the head of the lioness. Joshua could see the outline of her head and ears and, from where they stood, it looked as if the path lead straight into the open mouth. This was not a man made sculpture but the shape of the rock was unmistakably recognizable as the head of a lioness.

Grey and Krieg slowed down as they now stood almost directly below the upper part of the mouth. Joshua estimated that it was at least eight stories above him and from here it was nothing more than a large overhang in the cliff. In front of them, in the shadows, lay the pond. It was covered in lily pads. The blue color they had seen from the distance was not water, but the surface of the lily pad leaves which emitted a dark blue hue. As they entered the mouth of the lioness, Joshua realized immediately that there was no visible entrance into the mountain itself. Where the pond ended was a slight mound going uphill until it met the rock in the back of the mouth. The rock itself was smooth like the rest of the Wall. There was no indication of an entrance whatsoever.

Joshua flew off Krieg's back as they walked around the pond. The sound of a single peeper frog was the only thing they heard. They looked closely at the surface of the rock but there was absolutely nothing there. Joshua couldn't even begin to think of where to start looking. It would take days, weeks even.

"Maybe we have to go back and into the spider holes," the wolf's thoughts cut through the silence. "That might be the only entrance. Deep underground."

"If this is what it takes, what are we waiting for?" Krieg's thoughts were filled with impatience.

"No, Krieg. There must be a way. We came this far. I do not believe that we should go back to the holes of the spiders." Joshua tried to sound convinced, much more so than he was in truth. "The entrance must be here somewhere. We just have to find it."

Joshua began to walk along the Wall looking for any sign of a door, an opening, something out of the ordinary. Grey sniffed the ground around the pond. Krieg seemed to have lost all hope of ever finding it. He stood, his head low, waves of misery radiating from him.

"If we do not find it," he thought to them, "all of this was for naught. Everything we did up until now will have amounted to nothing. And I wish I would have died at the hands of my captors before you found me. For that is how I feel in my heart."

Joshua looked at his friend and felt his heart break for him. Grey walked over and lay down next to Krieg. Joshua did the same. There was nothing to say. All three of them felt the other's pain, felt the sudden end to their journey come nearer with every breath they took. Joshua dreaded the possibility that they would have to go through the spider holes. But maybe it was the only way into the mountain. He let the thought stand in his mind for a moment to see if it would gain strength.

"There is a way in."

Neither of the three reacted at first. They were too immersed in their despair.

"And I know it."

"What was that?" Grey thought to them.

"I heard it too," Joshua replied.

"I thought it was you, Joshua," Krieg thought.

"It wasn't me," Joshua answered.

"If it wasn't you, who was it?" Grey got up.

"It was me."

The three of them looked around. The thought was quiet, not so much a whisper but rather from someone who was very far away.

"Can you hear me?"

Neither of them could see anything.

"Where is this coming from?" Joshua thought. "Hello?"

"Would you please tell the mighty war horse not to move his front hooves? I'm right next to them and I do not wish to be trampled."

Joshua walked over to Krieg and looked around his hooves. Krieg's head was down and he was sniffing the grass.

"Here you are." It was Grey who found him first.

It was the peeper frog. He sat next to one of the horse's front hooves. He was so small, the three of them had to come very close to see him.

"You must be either very young or you are just very small," Joshua thought to him.

"I am neither," the peeper replied, looking up at them. "I am neither young nor small. For I am Broga, the guardian of the Porte Des Lioness."

"How old are you, Broga?" The wolf asked. "If I may ask."

"If you must know and I know you must, Grey, wolf from the Ice Forests, I was present when Alda was born."

The three of them looked at each other in disbelief.

"She was born right here in this pond under the protection of the lioness. I saw her fight her way through the thick shell of the egg she grew in. In fact I heard her singing before she came out of it. She sang then and she has never since stopped singing."

Joshua felt hope returning into Krieg's heart and into his own. He had no explanation for this. Nevertheless, this tiny little peeper had, within moments, given them back all the hope they had lost.

"Why should I not give you hope, my feathered friend?" The tiny frog looked up at them. "Have not you given hope to some, much larger than yourself? Hope does not judge your size and neither should you. Never doubt, *never* doubt that anyone with a fierce belief in his own destiny can't reach for the stars, as far away as they might seem to be."

Grey was the first to break the silence induced by Broga's thoughts. "The vulture has captured the Pegasus, and the spiders she has resurrected have brought her deep into the mines below Storm

Mountains. She demanded from us the exchange of the Pegasus for Joshua. We cannot agree to this, but we will and we must find Wind and free her and with her complete our journey to find the three feathers. For my friend has set out to find them and we have agreed to help him in his quest."

All was quiet. All eyes were on Broga, the little frog, who looked from one to the other.

"Since the mines were sealed by the sky people, no one has entered them and it has been my task to guard the entrance since then."

"How can the vulture get access to the mountain if she cannot come through here?" Krieg asked.

"The entrance was sealed so that no one was able to ever enter the mines again." Broga's thoughts were quiet, as if what he had to say was too important to be thought louder. "This gate, the Porte Des Lioness, was for the living. But in order to seal the entrance for the living, another entrance had to be opened … And that one is only for the dead."

It took a few moments for them to grasp what this meant, what this would mean.

"Are you saying that in order for Wind to be brought into the mountain, she has to be dead?" Krieg's calm thought betrayed the sense of despair that welled up inside him.

"Yes."

The finality hit Joshua full force.

"We should try to get to her before the vulture takes her through the gate," Krieg thought.

"I do not think this wise," Broga answered. "For you will never reach them in time and if they are through the gate already, then you cannot pass through it yourself. You would have to come back here and then you would have lost too much time."

"Broga, can you show us the way into the mountain?" Joshua asked.

The peeper looked at them. "I have been guarding this gate for over a thousand years. It has since then never been opened."

"Has anyone ever asked you to open it?" Joshua asked.

There was a pause.

"Broga, has anyone ever asked you to open the gate before?"

"No. No one has ever asked me. Many have come here in their search for the entrance but left a few days later."

"Because they didn't know it was right here. They didn't know the entrance was only visible from the Refuge and only if you were to stand right between the eyes of the lioness looking through the westerly window and beyond the small crack in the glass. No one knew where the Porte Des Lioness was. The ones before us were only guessing. Am I right? Broga, am I right?"

"Yes."

"THEN TELL US HOW TO GET INTO THE MOUNTAIN!" Joshua was surprised over the strength of his outburst. "We cannot wait any longer. You MUST show us the entrance. Too much is at stake and we are worthy... Are we not? We are worthy." With that last sentence Joshua seemed to collapse into himself. As if once he had thought the words, he no longer could believe them.

"You are worthy, Joshua. We are worthy," Grey thought to them.

"We are worthy," Krieg thought quietly.

There was silence. The thoughts echoed for a while in each of them. They had never spoken them like this before, never dared to. There was still a part within them that did not believe this to be true, but they did not have a choice. They needed to believe they were worthy. Joshua looked at his companions and saw the same determination in them that he felt in himself.

"I will show you the entrance, Joshua from the Great Lake," Broga thought to them. "And I will open it for you. But you must know that once you are inside the mountain, there is no way back for you. You must face whatever awaits you inside. You cannot go back for I will neither be able to hear you nor will I be able to open the gate more than once. You must realize this and fully. If you do, I will open the gate for you right now.

"Do it," Grey thought.

"Open it now," Krieg replied.

"I want you to open it, Broga, Guardian of the Gate. In the name of the lioness I want you to open the door into the mountain," Joshua answered.

There was a pause that in Joshua's mind seemed to stretch into infinity. Too much hung in the balance for them to fail now. The stakes were too high for them not to succeed.

"So be it." The frog's thoughts reached them quietly.

With that, Broga hopped in between Krieg and Grey and up the incline toward the Wall. Joshua and the others followed slowly. When the peeper reached the Wall he went along it feeling with his hands for something in the stone. Then he stopped. It was hard to see exactly but it seemed that he pushed against the wall and a tiny piece of the rock moved inward. It looked like a door that was barely high enough to let the peeper stand up in. It was miniscule. Broga entered. What occurred next was as astounding as it was unbelievable. It looked as if the tiny peeper pushed against the rock. Nothing seemed to happen at first. Then suddenly a straight vertical crack appeared above the peeper that went up at least ten feet. Broga pushed. And now the entrance moved. It was a massive slab of solid rock. The little peeper pushed it and it seemed to slide to the side leaving an opening.

Joshua was the first to enter. He realized that the gate was as thick as it was wide, solid granite. The tiny peeper moved the boulder and even though Joshua could see the strain in Broga's features, he could not believe that he was actually able to push it. Grey entered next, followed by Krieg. When the three of them were inside, they watched as Broga slowly pulled the gate closed. There were no good byes. When the door shut and it once again became invisible as if it had never existed in the first place, Broga sat down outside under the head of the lioness at the edge where the earth met the stone and thought about his life and what he had accomplished. He had opened the gate to the one who was destined to enter the mountain. He had fulfilled his life's purpose. He closed his eyes and became very peaceful. After a few minutes he drifted off and fell into a deep sleep from which he never woke up.

18. Submerged

*T*here was no sound when the door closed. Joshua expected it to be pitch black but instead there was a slight glow that emanated from the surface of the tube-like tunnel they stood in. It was just high enough for Krieg to walk upright. Its surface was smooth and solid, similar to the outside of the mountain. Joshua followed the tunnel with his eyes but could not see the end of it. It disappeared far into the distance.

"Are you ready?" Grey asked.

"No," Joshua answered truthfully and began to walk into the tunnel.

There seemed to be a slight downward pitch to it. The sound of their steps on the ground echoed through the semi darkness as they made their way ever deeper into the mountain. If the others had any thoughts they kept them to themselves. Krieg was limping slightly. The deep oozing cuts from the vulture had gotten more infected and Joshua was afraid the infection would spread the longer they walked. The low glowing that came from the surface of the stone around them illuminated the wounds and made them appear almost black. Krieg also couldn't lift his head as the height of the tunnel didn't allow it. Grey seemed fine. Nose to the ground, he concentrated on picking out any smells he could detect.

Joshua had lost all sense of time. He couldn't tell if they had been walking for hours or just minutes. His talons began to hurt. The smooth granite was hard and unforgiving. He began to feel thirsty. He hoped they would get through this tunnel soon even though he had no idea what to expect on the other side.

"There is water ahead," the wolf proclaimed. And only a short while later they came to a large puddle. Joshua gratefully drank from it. The horse and Grey did the same. While he drank Joshua looked down the long tunnel. He realized something that almost made his heart stop.

"Grey, how far can you see down into the tunnel?" He asked quietly.

Grey looked ahead, so did Krieg. The three of them saw it at the same time. The surface of the water mirrored the slightly glowing ceiling. The further they looked into the tunnel the closer the surface seemed to come to the ceiling. Far in the distance the surface of the water and the ceiling met. From then on the tunnel was submerged.

Joshua's heart sank. He looked at his companions. But before he could form a clear thought and communicate it with the others, Krieg began to walk into the water.

"Jump on my back, red one. There is no use standing here. Forward is the only way to go."

Joshua flew on the horse's back. He had to drop his head and crouch down so he wouldn't scrape along the ceiling. Grey began to swim next to them. Joshua watched him. Was this where their journey together would end? In a tunnel somewhere deep inside a mountain? Fear crept up inside him, tightening its grip around his chest. He had almost drowned twice. It was probably the worst experience of his life and he did not look forward to experiencing it again. As they drew closer to the point where the water met the ceiling, he tried to push away the overwhelming feeling of sickness that welled up in him. He had trouble breathing.

"Joshua," Grey had a tendency to interrupt his thoughts at exactly the right time. "I will go first and see what's down there and come back. Krieg will not be able to turn around in there."

Before Joshua could give any thought to this, Grey disappeared into the blackness. The horse's head stuck out of the water just enough for him to breathe. They waited. And waited. After what must have been an eternity Joshua couldn't take it any longer.

"I will be right back," he thought to the horse and with that, he jumped. Once under water, he began to use his talons to push forward but remembered very quickly that they were useless down here. The water was pitch black. The light on the tunnel's surface was completely swallowed up by the water. He felt a moment of panic, but then he became very still. It was as if his mind stopped its activity. He forgot about the question of what would happen if he didn't find an air pocket somewhere. He stopped thinking about Grey and he stopped thinking about his own life. And suddenly it was very clear to him. It was clear that he could do only one thing now. He opened his wings and pushed them downward and back, moving his body forward. After a couple of strokes, Grey appeared in front of him. His thoughts were panic stricken.

"Follow me!" Joshua told him.

He turned and swam back to where he came from. He felt the wolf behind him but the connection to him was fading fast.

"We're almost there, Grey, hold on!" He thought as he came up from the water. The wolf barely made it and when Krieg realized that Grey was in trouble he put his head under the wolf's belly and pushed him upward. The wolf hung there, miserably trying to get air into his lungs but he was alive and that was all that counted at the moment. Joshua realized that he was able to somehow keep his head above water. At least for now.

"I'm going back," Joshua thought.

"No, Joshua. Let me rest a while and I'll go back." Grey replied, still gagging from the water in his lungs.

"You can't go, Joshua. It's too dangerous," Krieg added.

"There is no other way. I will try to reach you. Keep your mind open."

Joshua went under. He figured he would do five strokes with his wings and see where this got him. If he didn't see anything he would turn back. He looked for some light or at least a glow indicating that part of the surface of the tunnel walls were not under water. When he was at the sixth stroke of his wings, he decided to turn around. He thought he did but it was so dark that he didn't see at all where he was going and suddenly he slammed into the tunnel wall. Panic rose in him. He was uncertain which way to go. He decided to go left thinking that this was the way back to the others. Four more strokes, but he still couldn't see anything. Two more and he felt that his lungs were about to burst. The blackness around him was complete and he tried desperately not to panic. But it was too late. A wave of dizziness enveloped him. His last wing stroke was already very weak. The impulse to take a breath was overwhelming. Before he passed out he saw a glimpse of a low glow in front of him.

He came back to life lying on the horses head. He couldn't breathe at first but then he realized that he wasn't under water anymore and that he could take a deep breath and fill his lungs with air. At the same time it occurred to him that they weren't back where they had started from. His head was close to the ceiling. Grey was treading water next to him. They were inside an air pocket that barely fit the three of them. There was a small space between the water's surface and the tunnel ceiling.

"How did you get here?" Joshua asked.

"We couldn't let you go by yourself," Grey answered.

"We certainly couldn't," Krieg added. "Try to hold on to my back. If I let the air out of my lungs I can walk under water. We must be about half way between where we started and the other side."

"I hope so." Joshua was not convinced. He felt numb and weak. He just wanted to rest and escape the feeling that they were buried inside a tunnel deep inside a mountain.

They waited a few more minutes to catch their breath. There was no turning back from here. They would either make it onto the other side together or they wouldn't. It was as simple and as terrifying as that. When Krieg let Joshua gently into the water he felt the cold seep into his body. Then the horse's head disappeared and Joshua went under. The wolf was first. Joshua held on to the horse's back as much as possible, thankful to have Krieg there with him. He knew they only had a very limited window of time and only one shot at this. There was a certain rhythm to the horse's movement that was very reassuring. At least for a while. Until Joshua realized that the horse was in trouble. It felt like a convulsion in Krieg's back. The strain of walking under water and the fact that he had to let out half of the air in his lungs weakened him rapidly.

"...can't hold breath much longer...," was what Joshua heard. A second convulsion went through Krieg's back. Joshua couldn't distinguish anymore between his own and the horse's dizziness and the attempt to squeeze every ounce of air they had out of their lungs got weaker and weaker every second.

"LIGHT!" Grey shouted in his thoughts. And then they saw that the surface of the water mirrored the glowing walls of the tunnel ahead. Part of Joshua's mind registered that Krieg's movement had slowed down. He was about to lose consciousness. If that happened, the horse would most certainly drown.

"Krieg, we're almost there. You can make it!" With that, Joshua dug his talons into the horse's back and with his last ounce of strength pushed his wings backwards. Once. Twice. They moved slowly toward the light. One more time and the horse's head came out of the water. Joshua let go and came up as well. They swam as quickly as they could to the water's edge and when Joshua reached it he looked back and saw that Krieg had collapsed. Only his head was out of the water, resting on the stone. The wolf stood there shivering miserably.

"Are you okay, Krieg?" Joshua thought.

For a while there was no answer, other than the massive chest of the horse moving up and down as he labored for breath.

"Krieg, are you going to be alright?" Joshua was too weak to move.

"I will be okay," Krieg's thought reached Joshua faintly. "I will be okay."

Joshua's last thought, before he fell into a deep and dreamless sleep was of Alda and of how she possibly could have known that a rooster needed so desperately to learn how to swim under water.

* * *

For a long time there was darkness. Wind could feel the bodies of the spiders under her when they carried her deep underground. Through tunnels that have never seen the sun, through ancient passage ways that never ended. The sound of hundreds of feet crawling over the ground, dampened by the web that was tightly wrapped around her head was the only thing she heard. She could hear the spiders' feet far ahead and far behind her as they brought her deeper and deeper toward their lair. They did not stop. They did not rest. As if lead by an invisible command that left them no choice but to respond, they carried their precious cargo until they reached their destination.

The cave was not very high but expansive in length and width. Its floor and ceiling had sharp, spear like crystals sticking out of them. Most of the crystals were covered in spider webs. There was a light source somewhere whose origin Wind could not determine. It illuminated the bizarrely shaped growths and cast long shadows on one side of them. The stench that lay in the air was of acid and decay and the unthinkable.

The massive vulture sat on one of the jagged pillars, her head cocked to one side. Below her sat two of the hyenas. One had half of her fur missing. It was scraped off exposing the raw skin and flesh down to several partially decomposed ribs. Her dead eyes were blood shot. Small veins stood in the sclera and what had once been white had taken on a yellowish tone. The other had flesh and skin hanging from her jaw bone and worms crawling in and out of what was left of her ear. Her teeth were bared revealing black gums.

As fast as the spiders had wrapped Wind in their first encounter on the surface, they now loosened her ties with hundreds of pincers tearing through the silken thread until all of it was gone except one thick piece tied around each wing and secured to one of the crystalline growths. When she stood up a wave of dizziness washed over her. Her legs weak, she had trouble standing. Spiders covered the ground and ceiling as far as she could see. At least a dozen of them sat right above her, their eyes peering at her waiting for the smallest command from their master.

"We meet at last," the vulture's thoughts brought with it the full impact of her malice. Wind could not escape the darkness, hopelessness and despair they induced in her. She felt utterly alone.

"Yes!" The vulture exclaimed triumphantly. "Alone is what you are and far from home. So far that never again will you reach its comfort, never again stand on familiar ground, never again touch kinship or brotherhood. It will forever be outside your reach. And death will only claim you once you have realized that even then peace will never find you. You will always be searching it even in the afterlife."

The vulture jumped from her perch and landed in front of her. She was a head taller than Wind even on equal ground.

"I will lay the marks of death upon your soul and it will burn with them. The poison will sink deep into it and there it will fester and make it its home."

The vulture's head was now close to Wind's. Her one dead eye looked into hers and suddenly the vulture let out a loud cry. At the same time she screamed at Wind in her thoughts. Wind moved backwards, trying to avoid her gaze. For an instant Wind thought she saw the slightest hint of fear in the vulture.

"LET ME EASE YOUR PASSING THROUGH THE GATE!" The vulture screamed. With that she jumped onto the back of the Pegasus and dug her talons deep into her skin. Wind's screams echoed through the subterranean lair. They never reached further than that.

* * *

Joshua thought that he must have slept for quite some time for when he opened his eyes his feathers were almost dry. Krieg stood a few feet away looking down at him. Grey sat on the other side.

"How long did I sleep?" Joshua shook himself. Besides a chill that still lingered, he felt surprisingly good.

"For a while," Grey replied. "We all did. And now we should get out of here."

"Well said," Krieg added.

They began to walk away from the water and up the slight incline of the tunnel. Joshua saw that Krieg's cuts from the vulture looked much better. The infection seemed to have gone completely and the wounds were beginning to heal.

"You are healing well," he told the horse.

"Yes. I feel much better. The pain in my side is gone almost completely," Krieg replied.

"There must be something in the water that counteracts the vulture's poison," the wolf remarked. Grey's thought stirred the somber memory of their captured friend in them. They all, in one way or another, tried to keep the thought of Wind's fate away from their hearts. The place where it would lead them was too dark, the sorrow over what would become of her too deep. But as much as they tried, they could not escape the gruesome images their imagination bestowed on them. Joshua could only hope that the images were wrong and just a cruel trick his mind played on him. Krieg who had experienced the vulture's razor sharp talons first hand took it especially hard.

They walked in silence for a long time until the light slowly began to increase. Its source came from the end of the tunnel. It lay still in the distance but was now visible as a small opening that grew larger the closer they came. When they reached it and stepped through it onto a plateau that was covered in thick green moss, they could not believe their eyes.

The platform they stood on was suspended above a deep chasm. Far below and to their right, a waterfall disappeared into the darkness. The falls were illuminated by a beam of light from high above. On the other side of the crevasse across from where they stood was another platform similar to this one. Beyond it was an opening leading further into the mountain. Both platforms had a narrow tongue of stone reaching toward each other. The middle part was missing. There was gap easily fifty yards wide.

The three friends stood at the edge looking across, dizzied by the sheer drop. They could not see the bottom of the abyss. Joshua thought that he would very possibly be able to make it to the other side. He had gained some strength in his wings since he had left the pen. Krieg should be able to make it also. But there was no way the wolf could.

"Why don't you two go? I'll stay," Grey thought to them.

"We can't leave you here," Krieg replied.

"You can't stay here with me either. That would do nobody any good. You have to go and find Wind, Krieg. And you have to fight the Vulture and get her back. I will be happy to stay here knowing that you will find her and free her." The wolf's thoughts hung there like a sword, Joshua felt. He could not imagine going on without Grey by his side.

"Do not be concerned with me, red one. For you have yet to find your full strength and go far beyond yourself. You will not be able to do this if you stay here."

"I do not wish to find strength within me if this means not to walk with you on my side."

"I will walk with you, Joshua. There will never be a day in which I will not walk with you. But now you must go."

Joshua heard the wolf's thoughts, but their meaning did not sink in. They stayed on the surface without much impact on him. He could not fathom losing his companion and he would rather stay here and starve to death before he would leave him.

"Joshua, if you stay here then all is lost. Wind will have died in vain. We all will have died in vain. You must go. I beg of you." Grey's thoughts were unyielding.

Joshua looked at him then he slowly retreated from the edge and went backwards toward the tunnel.

"Don't be so stubborn! You cannot hold off the inevitable!" The wolf's thoughts were loud and powerful in his mind accompanied by a low snarl. Joshua realized that he meant what he thought completely.

"I cannot, Grey. If this is the end of the journey for you it is the end for me as well."

"Then you are responsible if Krieg does not find Wind. Do you want this? Do you want to prevent him from seeing his beloved again?"

"No. I do not wish to see him suffer. But neither do I wish to see you die alone with no one but yourself to comfort you!"

"We all go or none of us does." Krieg's thoughts reached them both, abruptly ending their quarrel.

"You make no sense, war horse," the wolf replied angrily.

"And you must learn that you will never again be left behind," Krieg answered.

There was a moment of silence during which they looked at each other, seeing in one another what they could have never dreamed of before they began this journey. They knew at that moment that whatever happened, their friendship would abide.

"Here is what we will do." There was a warrior in Krieg that he thought had been lost in endless battles with no purpose. He fought his way to the surface for now he found something he could fight for and believe in. And when this purpose rose inside him, the warrior stood up and took control. "Grey, jump on my back. I will carry you to the other side. Joshua, you will follow us once we have landed safely there."

Without waiting for an answer, he went to the edge and unfolded his wings, testing their strength with several powerful strokes. "Come now, wolf, and do not think twice on it."

Joshua looked at Grey who met his eyes. He nodded slightly. The wolf turned and trotted back ten yards. He stood there for a moment and then charged forward toward the horse. When he jumped, Krieg pushed his massive wings down and when the wolf landed on Krieg's back he lifted off.

For a moment they hovered there. Then they dropped like a stone. Joshua saw them disappear below the ledge. He ran toward it and when he got there and looked over the rim, they were far down already, dwarfed against the blackness of the abyss. He saw Krieg's wings move, working against the fall, the sound of it echoing eerily through the cave. Fear gripped Joshua's throat. He thought about plunging after them but he heard Krieg's faint thoughts that told him unmistakably to stay where he was. Joshua felt absolutely powerless, unable to watch them and unable to look away.

How long is an instant? How long can it stretch out? For Joshua this one felt like an eternity. Until slowly, too slowly, the horse gained height.

"You can do it, Krieg"! He thought to himself over and over again. "Don't give up! Please!"

Joshua tried, as if by the sheer power of his mind, to lift his friends up and carry them to safety. There was an instant, just before they made it to the other side, when Joshua saw in the horse's eyes that he fought for his life and the life of the wolf, only a few feet below the ledge. His strength had left him, but he still pushed on trying desperately to gain the last short distance to safety. And then Joshua saw the wolf jump off and land on the other side. Krieg followed, collapsing right where he landed.

"Come to us!" Joshua heard Krieg's thoughts. Grey looked at him across the gap. Joshua could see the terror still looming in his face.

He peered down into the abyss. The light wasn't able to penetrate the darkness far below. Joshua's heart pounded against his chest. Krieg lifted up his head. "Do it now, Joshua."

Joshua knew that if he were to think about this he would lose all hope of ever doing it. So he locked eyes with Grey and pushed off, his wings unfolding. He tried not to look down but it was as if a magnetic force pulled his glance downward.

"Stay with me!" Grey demanded. And Joshua did. The wolf's eyes became his guide and he flew across the large gap and landed safely on the other side.

19. Ambushed

They rested for a short while with Joshua sitting close to Krieg who lay on the mossy ground until he gained some of his strength back. At length, they got up wordlessly and walked into the round opening of the second tunnel. None of them looked back.

The tunnel went a relatively short distance into the mountain and after a steep incline ended in another round opening that spilled them out onto grass. It didn't register right away as they stepped onto it. What they saw now was so strange it was hard to accept at first. Before them, a valley extended as far as they could see. There were soft rolling hills, green and lush. A distance away they saw what looked like a settlement of small houses tucked into the landscape. Dotted throughout the valley stood massive pillars of rough cut stone reaching far up and toward a ceiling that was so high above them it was hard to make out at all. The stone pillars were easily two hundred yards in diameter. The same light source they had seen in the other cave–or at least Joshua surmised that it was the same–illuminated parts of the landscape like a sun that stood low on the horizon. There were areas that lay deep in the shadows and others that were flooded with light.

A slight mist hung in the air giving the image in front of them an otherworldly quality. The small path in the grass led away from them and far down into the valley. It meandered through the hills reflecting the light like a thread of silver and ending in what must have been an ancient mining town during the time when the mountain was still harvested for rare crystallite. That was more than a thousand years ago.

They walked away from the pillar and onto the path. When Joshua turned around he saw that the landscape behind them extended an almost equal distance as it did in the front. He realized that the exit from the second tunnel was through one of the massive pillars. Joshua, Krieg and the wolf were awe struck by the magnificent scope of the land before them. It felt as if a force of great power had created this, a cataclysmic event of enormous magnitude occurred here in ancient times, millennia before the mining operations began. Joshua suddenly felt very small in relation to the landscape around him. He could sense that there was something larger at work here and he saw himself as just a tiny cog in a huge machinery that turned irrevocably, pushing him in a direction he was no longer sure he wanted to go.

The further they moved away from the pillar the larger it seemed. It became clear to them that the distance to the ruins of the mining town was much further than they thought at first. But having survived the last few hours had lifted their spirits and they made good time as they traveled down the path and through the hills below.

"This is odd," Grey remarked when they were about half way down the path between the tunnel and the town.

"What is it? Joshua asked. He sat on Krieg's back. They had decided that it would be easier if Joshua traveled the longer distances on the horse's back rather than trying to walk and keep up with the speed of the other two.

"The source of the light is constant," the wolf answered. "Since we came here it has not moved. I'm just wondering how long it will stay this way."

Joshua agreed with Grey. He, too, had had the brief and fearful thought that it would, at some point, just go dark. But he pushed the thought away. No sense playing the game of what if. Living through the ordeals of their journey, had helped steel him against thoughts like this.

At least he was able to keep them at bay for the most part. That in itself was new to him.

When the mining town came closer they saw that some of the houses were still intact. The path they were on had become a road that eventually would lead into the town center. From it, smaller roads branched off in both directions. The cluster of buildings extended into the hills that surrounded the town. There was a small stream that ran parallel to where they walked. It disappeared underground a little further down the road only to appear again close to the center of the town.

"It is so quiet here," Krieg remarked. "It seems there is no one in here other than ourselves."

"No one that lives, anyway," Grey answered. He immediately realized the meaning of what he had said. "I'm sorry, Krieg, I didn't mean… I did not want to burden you more with thoughts of Wind—"

"Do not concern yourself with it, Grey. I have a sense that she may still be alive after all," Krieg answered. Joshua and the wolf exchanged a brief glance. They saw it in each other's eyes that Krieg was the only one who believed the Pegasus was still among the living.

Quietly they walked the rest of the way until they passed the first houses. Most of them had no roofs. Blind windows peered at them. The stone with which they were built was crumbling and overgrown with vines. Some of them had thick layers of moss growing on them. When they stopped for a moment to rest at the small creek they realized that aside from the slow running water of the stream, there was absolutely no sound whatsoever. It was eerily quiet. And when they continued toward the center and the creek disappeared underground, the sound of Krieg's hooves on the road echoed through the abandoned streets like a reminder that as vast as this cave was, they were alone. Until Joshua became aware of them.

Out of his peripheral vision he saw a shadow move between two buildings. It was low to the ground and fast and gone when he looked again. Then there was another further down the road. Joshua looked at the wolf.

"I saw it," Grey's thought was quiet.

"What do you think?" Joshua answered as quietly.

"How the hyenas made it into the mountain, I do not know," the wolf answered. "But they are here now. I counted four of them so far. Two on either side of us. Joshua, you stay with Krieg. I will take care of them."

Joshua was about to tell him that this certainly was not a good idea when Krieg's thoughts reached them. His were as quiet as their own. "I do not doubt you could take them, wolf, if they were among the living. But they are not. They are dead and not bound by the laws you and I believe in. You cannot take them but be assured that they *can* take you."

Grey looked at him. "What do you suggest?"

"We have to stay together!" Krieg answered. "That is our only chance to get out of this alive and in one piece."

There was no time for either of them to form another thought. The hyenas came at them from two directions. One came from between two houses and charged toward them. Grey, out of sheer instinct, charged toward her. At the same time another jumped out of a window that was near where Krieg stood. It took the horse completely by surprise. The hyena reached him before he could move. Her huge fangs open, she flew at him. Her teeth scraped his side before he went on his hind legs. That was probably what saved him. She couldn't grab on to his skin and let go for only an instant. It was enough for him to kick her with his front legs and she winced, retreating back a few feet.

The wolf wasn't as lucky. The hyena attacked him with all that she had and even though he was at least equal in strength and speed he was no match for her ferocity. Joshua realized that Grey wouldn't last very long. He flew off the horse's back and toward the wolf. He didn't know exactly what he was going to do except to somehow disturb the hyena's relentless attacks. So he landed on her back. It was not a place he wanted to end up, but he didn't have full control over his flying and landing skills. He dug his talons into the hyena's back and started pecking at her.

He wasn't sure if she even felt it but she turned her head once to see what was happening behind her. That was enough for the wolf to charge forward and grab the hyena by her throat. Under normal circumstances this would have killed her instantly. But even after his teeth had penetrated the skin and flesh, she showed no signs of slowing down. Her attacks just got more ferocious.

"I don't know how to kill her!" The wolf's panicked thoughts came fast. "Any ideas?"

In his periphery, Joshua saw the horse trample the hyena, kicking it several times but she just got back up and came charging at him again. This was a losing battle. The hyenas did not get tired and, as of right now, there were only two of them. Where the other two were he didn't even know.

The wolf did not back down but it seemed only a matter of time before he would need to catch his breath.

Suddenly the hyena stopped in mid attack and ran back up the road. The wolf charged after her.

"Grey, no!" Joshua thought. But the wolf was gone, disappearing between two houses. Joshua flew up onto one of the higher buildings then to another one and yet another. From there he looked down into a courtyard into which the hyena had just fled. He saw the wolf follow her. The moment Grey stepped into the courtyard which was surrounded on four sides by stone walls with a small opening through which they had come in, Joshua knew it. "It's a trap!" He screamed in his thoughts. "Get out of there!

As Grey turned, the other two hyenas entered. One came toward the wolf, the other waited at the entrance, guarding it and making sure he would not be able to get out. Joshua didn't think twice about it. He swooped down and went straight for the one at the entrance. As the two other hyenas closed in on the wolf, who was now cornered on the opposite side of the entrance, Joshua landed on the head of the third. He went straight for her eyes. That was the only thing he could think to do. The hyena tried to snap at him and the first couple of times Joshua was still able to hold on to her. But then she jerked her head to one side and he lost his grip. He crashed to the ground and lay before here. For an instant nothing happened. Suddenly his courage turned into utter panic and, terror stricken, he tried to get to his feet. The hyena turned her head toward him. Her blind eyes stared at him from above and he thought he saw her grin. Then her jaws opened to grab him.

In that instant, Grey rammed into her, pushing her to the ground. "Go!" He thought to Joshua and with that he fled behind the next house. As Joshua flew up he saw that the three hyenas charged after the wolf. He followed their path from the air. They reached the road and crossed it. The wolf ran through the stream which was surprisingly deep. It slowed him down enough for the hyenas to catch up. One of them went into the water with him; the others ran further down the road to a small foot bridge to cut the wolf off on the other side.

When Grey came out of the water he went in the opposite direction along the creek. The hyena closest to him followed him out of the water and ran after him. But suddenly something strange happened. When the hyena was just about to reach him, she fell to the ground. She got back up and ran a few more feet before she fell again. This time she just lay there. Grey looked back and couldn't believe what he had just witnessed. The hyena made one more feeble attempt to get up but then stopped moving altogether. She seemed to fall into herself until, after only a few more seconds, there was nothing left of her but fur flattened to the ground. And even that seemed to disappear rapidly into it the earth.

The other two hyenas didn't seem to notice and charged after Grey as ferociously as before. Just when the wolf began to run into a space between two houses, it occurred to Joshua.

"Water! It's the water, Grey! There is something in the water! You must lead them into the creek!" Joshua hoped that Grey could still hear him as he had already disappeared between two houses. But suddenly the wolf came racing back out and straight toward the creek. The two hyenas followed him into it without hesitation. They did not know. It occurred to Joshua that they had no idea what would cause their demise.

Grey jumped out of the water on the other side and ran straight toward Krieg who was still fighting the first hyena. Krieg saw the wolf pursued by the other two who suddenly lost their footings and fell, tumbling over several times before they stopped moving. Krieg knew instantly what he needed to do and charged toward the creek. The last hyena was hard on his tail when he went into the water. Krieg didn't bother coming back out. He just ran up the stream until the hyena stopped moving. Whatever was left of her body was washed away. The life that had temporarily been forced back into her was gently taken by the stream and so purified of all that was unnatural to her being. Death could finally claim her and her tortured soul found peace at last.

* * *

Far above them, unseen, unheard, and unnoticed, the vulture circled overhead, her blind eye peering down at them. Her hatred for the rooster intensified a thousand fold and she knew she would not rest until he lay before her on the ground, crumbling and begging for his life. She would take it from him and, in doing so, make hers last forever.

* * *

They stood shaking; the terror still clinging to their exhausted bodies. It was only slowly overtaken by the relief that they survived. Grey finally lay down in the middle of the road and began to lick his wounds. They were mostly superficial, but could get infected later on. Better to take care of them now. Joshua looked at Krieg's new scars. "The old ones haven't even healed yet," he thought, more to himself than to anyone else.

"They will heal, Joshua, as did all the others," the horse replied. Joshua found himself in awe of the war horse and the wolf and of what they had endured, were still enduring. Is this what friends do? Stay with you until the end? With no question, no complaint and with your safety the sole concern inside their thoughts and hearts? He did not believe it possible that friendship could reach such depths. He was humbled before it. He could not have conceived the riches this brought to him and he could not think of anything he wanted more in his life than this. Even his dream of the three feathers seemed dull in comparison. He thought at that moment that as much as he still wished to find them, if he were to be without his friends, he would not want the feathers, not for any price. He would rather stay with Grey and Krieg instead, wherever that might be.

They decided to rest for a short while. Wary of what lay ahead, Krieg insisted that they might need their strength, and all of it, before this was over. At first it seemed odd to Joshua that the horse did not want to charge forth and confront the vulture head on. But then he realized that Krieg, as much as he wanted to see Wind again, was frightened of the condition in which he would find her. It was an impossible situation for the horse and Joshua wished he could do something about it. Sometimes avoiding ones worst nightmares, he thought, seemed as daunting a task as confronting them.

During their brief rest, the wolf caught a few fish in the stream, Krieg grazed on a patch of grass and Joshua was able to still his hunger on what he found in the soft soil. As they walked out of the old mining town on the opposite side of where they had entered, Joshua considered that, under normal circumstances, the landscape here would probably be worth exploring. He wondered if the large pillars were cut by hand as part of the mining operation or if they had been here, built up over eons and eons of time. He also wondered about the light source and its origin. How had the hyenas come back to life? And the spiders? He had yet to lay eyes on the vulture. Only in frantic images that he received from Krieg had he seen her. Going toward what could easily be his own death was not something he looked forward to.

It was a somber walk through the valley for the three companions as they passed a seemingly endless number of pillars that rose from the ground far up toward an invisible ceiling. The light source receded into the distance behind them and, as they continued to move ever deeper into the massive cave, Joshua suddenly realized that it had gotten significantly darker. When they eventually climbed a small hill and stood on its crest looking forward, it appeared as if the massive cave ahead swallowed the light completely. A relatively small distance away from them, the path they were walking on disappeared into utter darkness.

"Grey, how far can you see into the cave?" Joshua asked.

"Not very far at all," Grey answered.

"I don't like this," Joshua added. The thought of not knowing where the next step would lead was frightening enough under normal circumstances. But they also had to think about the possibility of an ambush at any moment. Before Joshua could fully picture hundreds of glowing spider eyes in the dark before him, the wolf cut into his thoughts, reminding him once again not to go where he was about to go.

"I will be right next to you," the wolf's thoughts reassured him.

"And I will be on your other side," Krieg added.

"Then what are we waiting for?" He thought, looking up at them. The wolf smiled in his thoughts. Joshua took one hesitant step forward and then another and another after that. Grey and Krieg followed, taking their places on either side of him as they descended from the hill and rejoined the path. To anyone watching, it would have seemed as if they simply disappeared into the darkness.

20. Awakening

is sleep was deep and in it he created worlds beyond worlds and he went far into them and he lost himself in them. For centuries he slept, weaving dreams that spun in all directions. They took him to places of deepest darkness and brightest sunlight. He felt the winds of the plains take him and he flew high above the land and reached far beyond the stars. He sailed on solar winds through the emptiness of space. He watched whole civilizations come and go and rebuild themselves only to be destroyed again. He saw the summit of creation and he felt the depth of despair along with the heights of peace among men. He was free and the longer he slept the further his dreams took him. And he saw places so ancient they had existed before time and he glimpsed futures that had not yet been realized, but soon would come to life. Then he awoke.

He became aware of his deepest core first. He felt his heart beat against his massive chest. It transported his blood through silver veins— blood that was of darkest blue. One drop of it could kill all forms of life within a hundred yards. He began to feel the extension of his limbs, the cold in his extremities, the movement in his scales when air streamed into his lungs. He felt the heat of his breath as it scorned the air in front of him. When his eyes opened, his pupils adjusted to the light, deep green irises contracted into small slivers.

He saw everything at once: the beam of light that pierced the darkness from somewhere high above in the crystalline ceiling; the body of water to his left, its surface reflecting its surroundings in shimmering light; the blackened soil in front of him. He saw the claws in his powerful front talons that could cut into stone; that could carve pillars out of granite. He felt the power returning to his limbs and all the way to the tip of his leathered wings.

But something was wrong. He could not name it until he heard it. It was just a whisper at first, then two, then five, then a dozen voices murmuring, sighing in an ever returning rhythm. The whispers slowly turned into sounds, indistinguishable at first until they became small feet on charred ground, hairy limbs rushing against each other. The light. That was what was missing. It was too dark in here. The light source in the crystallite ceiling on one side of the cave was completely blocked. When his eyes looked up he saw them. And before he could command his powerful legs to push him off and to burn them into oblivion with his fiery breath, they descended upon him.

The spiders came and while they overtook his stirring body they wove their web and covered him with it. He fought them. He pushed off with his hind legs, extended his wings far to either side. He lifted off but only for an instant. From afar it was an image of terrifying beauty. In the semi darkness of the cave, the massive dragon fought for his life – fought to lift off the ground. But there were too many. The more that fell off of him, the more that jumped onto him from the ceiling. In the end he lost the battle and was soon covered in a web that left him no choice but to watch what was about to happen.

He saw the ivory coat of the Pegasus before he could see what she was. And when he did, when he saw the spiders carrying her while others built a web in the air between two pillars; and when they lifted her lifeless body up and fastened her to the web that spanned easily a hundred yards across; and when he saw her beauty in the beam of light that gently rested upon her he also saw the deep and dark red markings, the inflamed and festering cuts all over her body. When he saw it all he wept for her. And where his tears fell to the ground, penetrating the charred soil, small flowers began to grow in the darkness underground. And if someone would have visited the abandoned cave only a few years later she would have seen a sea of flowers covering the dragon's den and the area where he had slept.

But now there was only death. The dragon, who could no longer distinguish between his dreams and the lives before he slept, thought he remembered the Pegasus as they fled deep into the mountain a thousand years since passed. They were freed in the mines by a small group of sky people who had no choice but to seal the caves forever. He knew then, in an instant, the whole of Wind's past, what she thought was her betrayal of her own race and her subsequent choice to be petrified in stone until the mountain would take her or the elements would diminish her into oblivion.

And he saw her gaining her freedom, born out of the sheer pain of the war horse for her imprisonment. He saw the rooster and the wolf and through her he saw their companionship with each other. And what he had dismissed many lifetimes ago in exchange for an existence in solitude began to stir deep within him and thoughts of friendship and of the hope it brought came to him through her and it lifted his heart high above, even though his body was bound to the stone.

And he knew that she was alive. That the poison of the vulture had only slowed her heartbeat to a point of seeming death but that she still was there, faint perhaps and not for very much longer, but still alive. He held on to this thought. Lying there, tied with thousands of threads, held tight against the floor, he felt a surge of power coming through him. He thought that he would let it build up until he would no longer be able to contain it and then he would free her and himself, and his fury would know no limits.

At that moment the vulture landed in front of him. And when she looked into his eyes he could not help but see his own death and the shattering of all the hopes he ever held inside. And even though he could feel the life of the Pegasus slowly leaking out of her, he could not muster the strength to oppose the vulture's glance that told him unmistakably of his demise. But that was not what he was afraid of. What he feared the most was just one thing. And when he allowed the thought of it to come into his mind he knew it could not be undone. He knew the vulture saw it clearly within him. She would not kill him. She would leave him here in the darkness, alive. But she would take his dreams from him and she would exchange them for nightmares that would last for an eternity.

21. The Long Dark

The night came silently, overtaking Joshua and the others slowly as they walked along the path and into the blackness of the cave. In the beginning, they could still see the landscape around them. But soon all they saw was shadows within shadows. And then, from one moment to the next, all that was left was darkness. The wolf was the only one who was able to make out the faintest glow of the path ahead. Joshua and Krieg were blind, wrapped in darkness so complete, Joshua decided to close his eyes as it did not matter whether they were open or shut. He felt the coolness of the air around him and the warmth of Krieg's body beneath him. He heard the horse's hooves on the soil below and the wolf's slow trot but the sounds seemed to dissipate somewhere into the vastness of the cave.

Joshua was glad he had decided to fly onto Krieg's back when it was still light enough. It would have been impossible for him to do so now. Feeling Krieg's warm body under his talons gave him comfort at first, but then he began to feel the horse's nervousness. Not being able to see was something Krieg had always feared and Joshua received images from him of large crevasses ahead into which they could fall without warning. It began to make Joshua himself uncomfortable. Grey tried to reassure them that even though it was just a faint shimmer, he did see the path in front of them. But being told something and experiencing it were two completely different things. There was nothing to do but to trust that

Grey would see where they were going. They walked in silence along the darkening path until the rest of the light was swallowed up as well.

"I can't see anything anymore," Grey thought quietly to them. "Not ahead and not behind me." There was no warning in his thoughts. Just the simple recognition that they were now completely blind to their surroundings. "I just hope that whoever else is in here won't see anything either."

"Can you still sense the path, Grey?" Joshua asked.

"I think so. The ground seems to be getting sandier though. Soon, it will be hard to find the path at all."

The wolf's thought trailed off leaving them with a void that was soon filled with the dread of what lay ahead. From now on, every step brought with it the fear of it being their last. They walked for close to a day and did not want to stop even though they were exhausted, for each minute they spent in the dark without moving was a minute more that deprived them of the light. At some point they just couldn't walk anymore. They lay down and slept right there. When Joshua opened his eyes a few hours later, he was disoriented at first and sure he had gone blind.

"Grey?" He thought into the darkness.

"I'm here," the wolf answered. "The next half mile at least we are clear."

"You went ahead?" Joshua could not deny his concern for the wolf.

"Yes. I still have my nose, remember?"

"And we are glad for it," Krieg added. "Have you found anything beyond the path?"

"No. It dissolves into an open field of sand and rock. I'm afraid from there we won't have much to go on. Not much at all."

There was a moment of silence between them.

"But there is one good thing," Grey added.

"What's that?" Joshua asked.

"From now on, it can only get lighter."

Joshua saw the wolf smiling in his thoughts. Krieg made a noise that sounded much like laughter and Joshua couldn't help but smile as well. And for a moment there was light in their minds and the darkness that surrounded them didn't seem so impenetrable. And for a while they walked with certainty of step and with less fear inside their hearts. Twice they almost ran into one of the pillars. It was only the wolf's sense of what was in front that stopped them. Once Grey reported that they had passed a certain spot before and they realized that they had gone in a circle. They did not speak about this but they knew that they would not be able to keep this up much longer. Traveling in complete darkness through potentially treacherous terrain pulled on their strength and Joshua could feel the horse's exhaustion beneath him. Grey was always moving ahead, nose to the ground and trying to find a scent of something that could help. But he was approaching the end of his endurance as well.

When Joshua was close to suggesting that they give up, they heard a sound. They couldn't pinpoint its location at first and went in the wrong direction, moving away from it. Soon they found they could not hear it at all and they had to turn around until the sound came back. After a while it got louder and they could sense where it came from more clearly. They could not contain their relief. It was water. A small trickle, possibly a brook, maybe even the continuation of the stream they had encountered in the mining town. When they reached it they all took a long time to still their thirst. Joshua did not realize how thirsty he was until he had water. For a while they did nothing but drink, taking in the cold, fresh elixir of life.

"We can follow it," Grey suggested. "At least while it flows on the surface."

They all agreed and they walked along the stream for what must have been half a day until it was suddenly gone again. It silently disappeared underground and with it, its comfort left them as well. For the last hour before that, Joshua had gotten bits and pieces of strange images. From where he did not know. They were incomplete and most of them were undecipherable. But subsequently one image appeared that was so clear and so strong, Grey and Krieg saw it at the same time: There was a light beam coming from high above. It illuminated a large spider's web that was spun between two pillars. Wind's lifeless body was tightened into the web. She was covered in blood from deep cuts all over. Krieg's first impulse to run toward her—wherever that might be—was only countered by the wolf's and Joshua's strong plea not to do so. Finally, the horse gave in.

"We have to be careful about this," Grey explained. "Obviously this is a trap and designed to create exactly the reaction you just had, Krieg. We don't know where the images came from. Joshua, do you think they stem from the vulture?"

"I wouldn't know. The image of Wind wasn't the only one I got. There were others and they were strange and... otherworldly. Like remnants of dreams someone had. Now that I think of it, I do not believe these are the vulture's dreams."

"Why do you think that?" Krieg asked.

"Because they were filled with joy," Joshua answered.

"Was there anything else you saw?" Grey asked.

Joshua thought for a moment. It took him a while to sift through the chaotic images but there was one partial image he got that now came back to him. It was that of a large body of water that seemed to be on the periphery of the image that showed Wind in the spider web. When he told Krieg and Grey about it they were both quiet for a moment.

"We must guard our thoughts about this," the horse thought. "We cannot think of this again. It might be the only chance we have to fight the vulture. We have to somehow get her into the water."

"If there is water, there might still be hope for Wind as well. If we get her into it, she might come back to life." Krieg's thoughts spoke of hope—a hope Joshua did not share. He was certain the Pegasus was dead. He kept his thoughts about it as quiet as possible but he knew that some of it must have been leaking out and Krieg probably had a sense of what he was thinking.

"I know your thoughts, Joshua," Krieg answered. "But I do not share them. I cannot. I dare not. If there is the slightest chance that she lives, I cannot think of her as dead. And I hope you will join me in this for I do not wish to sentence her to death in my thoughts."

"I'm… sorry, Krieg. I cannot help it. My thoughts will not leave me even though I try to push them away."

"Do not concern yourself for you have done nothing wrong. But guard your thoughts and guard them well for otherwise we will not stand a chance. Without the water we will have nothing to use against her."

"Then let us go now," Grey added. "And let us be swift."

The others agreed and for the next few hours they walked in silence and as fast as they dared through the blackness of the cave.

* * *

At first, Joshua thought it sounded like a wave. Then it turned into wind rustling through tree tops. Whatever it was, it came closer with immense speed and Joshua could suddenly feel Grey's coat stand up. They stopped where they were. A low snarl escaped the wolf.

"Brace yourselves!" Grey told them quietly.

The wave washed over them and for a moment it seemed to come from all sides. Then it stopped.

"What was that?" Krieg asked.

"I do not dare to think it, but I know," the wolf answered.

Joshua heard a low humming sound generated by the scraping of thousands of feet on the rocky ground. The spiders had surrounded them. Joshua sensed their dead eyes peering at them through the dark. They had left a small buffer between themselves and the area where Joshua and the others stood. For a moment nothing happened. The three friends didn't move; didn't dare to. But suddenly the spiders, as if lead by an invisible command, moved toward them from their left side. They had no choice but to go in the other direction. When Krieg and Grey started walking, the spiders began to move as well. The sounds their feet made echoed eerily through the vast blackness. Joshua shivered at the thought of being enveloped by countless bodies of large spiders in complete darkness.

While they travelled, Joshua realized that, even though this was an absolutely terrifying experience, he was relieved that at least they didn't have to worry about where to go anymore. The spiders lead them through the cave, correcting their path here and there by coming closer to one side of them until they adjusted where they were going. Joshua tried to make out what they thought or felt, but there was absolutely nothing there. It was emptiness that surrounded them – emptiness in thought and emotion. It was as if their bodies were propelled solely by the sheer force of the vulture's command. The souls of the spiders had left their hosts back in the cold of the Refuge. They had long since gone home to their ancestors. Whatever force drove them now, controlled their shells. Nothing more. There was no evil in them. None at all. It became clear to Joshua that, should the vulture fall, the spiders would go with her. Released from her command, they would just disintegrate and simply cease to be.

"I can see light." The wolf's thoughts interrupted his own. "Faint, still, and far in the distance, but there." Joshua hadn't known how much he dreaded this until Grey's thoughts reached him. He had longed for the light. After two days in absolute darkness, the light should have been the most welcome treasure for him. But it brought with it a whole litany of things that Joshua did not want to face—Wind's fate foremost among them. But another thought slowly made its way into his conscious mind. It was one he had avoided for as long as he could. It had, by now, finally caught up with him. It was the thought of his own death. He did not see much hope in their ability to defeat the vulture. She was just too powerful. Certainly he couldn't win against her. Krieg was no match against her talons in the air and the wolf had no chance against her even on the ground. And that was without the spiders. It seemed all but hopeless.

But there was, hidden and buried under all the others, another thought and one that demanded at least part of his attention. It was the thought of fighting her. It was the thought, as preposterous as it seemed at the moment, of fighting her with everything they had—with every ability and every ounce of strength that was still left in them. And for the smallest of moments he felt it, felt it rise within him and strengthen his resolve. For a moment he felt the presence of the lioness within him. It was faint and her full strength eluded him. But it was enough for him to straighten himself and to no longer crouch down. It was enough to tell Krieg and the wolf that they would not be defeated and that they would fight until the end and fight for each other and for the life of the Pegasus.

He could sense the others' silent approval but he could also sense, for a brief moment, a disturbance moving through the spiders. A slight interruption in their rhythm as if whatever had welled up in Joshua had somehow affected them. Was it fear he felt from them? But that couldn't be. They were dead. There was neither fear nor hatred or any emotion left in them. Was it possible that whatever he had felt inside had somehow been communicated through the spiders to the vulture? Was it her fear he sensed?

"Krieg, I want you to stay calm but I think I can see what's at the end of the cave." Grey's thoughts reached them quietly. And with it came an image that sent a shiver down the horse's spine. Joshua had to pull on all his strength to keep from letting out a loud crow. They saw Wind. She hung in the web illuminated by a single beam of light coming from somewhere high up in the ceiling. The cuts in her belly and side were dark red. If Joshua had any hope of her being alive before, it was taken from him at that moment. He could not hold on to it. It dissipated like a single spark in the night. What was left was hopelessness. The power the vulture had over them was too strong.

"Shield your thoughts, Joshua," Grey thought. "She can sense your fear and will give it back to you a thousand fold. You will not be able to fight her if you are held back by fear. We need you."

Joshua realized that he could see the wolf again. Not fully yet as the darkness was still too thick around them. But he could make out his silhouette and he saw Grey's eyes clearly when he looked back at him.

"You must reach deep down into yourself, Joshua. You must forget everything you have learned and you must become greater, stronger, and more than you think you are right now. Whatever you have felt inside you, up in the tower of Refuge, you must command it to you and you must hold it and not let go of it. You must command it, Joshua."

"I must command it," Joshua answered.

"You must command it!" The wolf's eyes wouldn't let go of his and Joshua couldn't turn away.

"I must command it," Joshua answered again.

The wolf nodded slightly. Then his eyes released Joshua's and he turned again toward the light and Wind's lifeless body that hung in its glowing beam.

22. Battle

The light beam extended its glow into the cave and Joshua could now see the spiders that surrounded them. Their numbers were far greater than he originally thought. There were hundreds of them, maybe thousands—their dark bodies partially illuminated by the glowing light. And then, suddenly, they left. The sound of their feet on the ground swelled up for a few moments and then dissipated into the shadows of the cave. And within a few seconds Joshua could not see any of them. They were gone. The quiet that returned left them with nothing but the image of the Pegasus in the web three hundred yards ahead.

It was too much for Krieg. "I must go to her!" He charged forward. Joshua lost his grip and flew off his back, landing next to the wolf on the ground.

"No!" Grey howled, its echo travelling through the massive cave. "She will use everything she knows against you!"

But it was too late. Krieg was already halfway there and he was going fast. His wings were partially extended as if he was about to lift off. The wolf didn't want to leave Joshua behind so he trotted slowly while Joshua ran and flew part of the way. Then they saw the horse reach the web. Joshua could hear Krieg's cries as he stood under it looking up at Wind. He went up on his hind legs, but still couldn't reach her. Joshua felt Krieg's utter desperation but this did not prepare him for what he felt when he actually stood next to the horse and looked up.

The Pegasus hung about thirty yards above them in a web that was easily one hundred yards wide and as tall. Her wings and part of her body were wrapped in a cocoon that was woven into the web. The red infected wounds stood out in stark contrast to her ivory coat. There was no sign of life in her.

"We have to get her down!" Krieg's thoughts were frantic with concern about her.

"We can't, Krieg," Joshua answered as calmly as possible.

"We have to get her down! She can't stay up there. We have to do something."

"There is nothing we can do for her right now," Grey added as calmly as he could. "Neither of us can even reach the web. Joshua could fly up there but he would get tangled in it and then both of them will be caught."

"No. I won't accept that," the horse answered. "There must be something we can do to help her—"

"And there is…"

The vulture swooped down silently and landed behind them. The wolf turned first. Joshua could sense the desolation he felt the moment Grey's eyes met hers.

"The great gray wolf from the Ice Forrest. What a mighty friend the rooster has chosen for his quest. And how much greater his defeat will be once he realizes the full extent of your weakness." The vulture's thoughts penetrated Grey's mind mercilessly. "I met your companion, wolf. At least what was left of her once the hunter was done with her remains. I commanded her to rise from the dead and she could not deny my request. Right now she roams the ice in search of her companion who has abandoned her for the rooster. As for you, you will die alone, wolf. And there will be no place for you to go where you will meet her again. You will have died for nothing but to feed my army, giving them life with your death. The one thing you will have accomplished is to bring the rooster to me. That will be your end. To give me eternal life in exchange for the rooster's. And to feed the dead with your own demise."

The wolf snarled and whined at the same time. His wincing echoed through the cave. Joshua was convinced that he was about to charge toward her any moment. But behind the vulture and out of the shadows two hyenas now stepped into the light. They were larger than the others, almost twice the size of the wolf. Their dead eyes spoke of blood and flesh hanging from bones and of a horrifying death.

"And you, Krieg." The vulture looked at the horse, black saliva dripping out of her half decomposed beak. "I will give you a war of such you have not yet dreamed of. A war that will be fought in your heart. For you will watch while I feed on the Pegasus' body and you will forever know that you did nothing to prevent me from doing so. That will be your enemy; the foe you will pursue for the rest of your life. It will be a war that will be fought inside you and you will be slain upon its altar each time you think of her. You will feel her pain and her love will escape you and comfort will never reach your restless soul."

Krieg was frozen. Unable to move, he stood facing the vulture. Every fiber of his being told him to attack her full force. But what he saw in her eyes made him want to hide somewhere instead. Krieg, possibly the greatest war horse of his time, was immobilized by fear and a terror so great he could do nothing but accept his defeat.

Joshua was privy to the wolf's and the horse's exchange with the vulture. While he looked at her he could feel death's unrelenting grip upon his throat. It was suddenly hard for him to breathe. He felt Krieg's terror and Grey's desperation as if they were his own, but through it all there was another presence he felt. It came from somewhere deep in the shadows of the cave. It was immense, its consciousness vast and its power almost limitless. At least under normal circumstances. But he felt that whatever it was, it was captive to the vulture's curse like Joshua and the others.

"Help me," the dragon whispered faintly in his thoughts. "Help me!"

And for an instant, Joshua could sense the magnitude of the nightmares it endured at the vulture's hands. They were nightmares spun of the dragon's dreams that once were of such beauty they would have made him weep. But now all the beauty was gone and what was left was perpetual hopelessness.

There was suddenly motion when the area beyond the reach of the light beam began to move. The spiders came back and crawled up the two pillars on either side of the web closing in on Wind. Their bodies crawled all over her and at first it looked like they were strengthening the cocoon. But then Joshua saw that the spiders untied her from the web and carried her down to the ground. Joshua and the others had to move otherwise they would have been overrun by the spiders who brought Wind's limp body to a predestined spot where they placed her on the stone. They disappeared as quickly as they came, back into the shadows of the cave.

And then it dawned on Joshua. The body of water was very close to Wind. When Joshua and Grey's eyes met for a moment, he knew that the wolf thought the same thing. Grey's reminder to guard his thoughts was in his eyes as well. If they could somehow get the Pegasus into the water she might come back to life. Joshua felt a spark of hope return to him—hope that they might have a chance after all. It was slim, perhaps, but a spark might be all they needed. A spark and a moment of surprise. If they were to charge at her all at once and somehow catch her before she could lift off... Joshua began to think that it was possible to defeat her.

Was it a grin he saw in her? He thought at first that his eyes played tricks on him. The vulture did not grin in the flesh. But he realized that she grinned within his mind. And her grin became laughter. It mocked them and the three companions looked at each other, not knowing what to make of it. Then it dawned on them. She knew about the water. And she knew that they knew. She had known since they had defeated the hyenas back at the village. She was playing with them, playing with their hopes, building them up only to crush them again.

"You are very perceptive, Joshua Aylong," he felt her pestilence wreaking havoc in his mind, searching it for every little scrap of thought she could use against him. It was over. And he was suddenly transported back to the day when the farmer took the other rooster from the pen and held him down on the ground to cut off his head and he felt the rooster's terror at that moment. He could not help feel responsible for his death and for every single soul that had perished before and after him. Joshua wanted to die at that moment. He wanted it all to end, wanted to just disappear into oblivion and nothingness and not experience the terror of this moment any longer. He looked at the wolf next to him who shook his head ever so slightly in a 'no'.

Then Grey, without giving any indication he would do so and in one fluid motion, charged toward the vulture who was, at that moment, about ten yards away from them. The large wolf gained speed fast and just before he reached her, she lifted off, mocking him with her laughter and loud cries. At the same time the hyenas moved toward the wolf, closing in on him and meeting him at the place where the vulture had just sat. Their fangs tried to dig into the wolf's neck but he was strong and quick and he avoided them and caught one of them by the throat. Normally the hyena would have died instantly. But she was already dead and nothing could kill her now. The wolf knew that. He pulled her toward the water. She was fighting him but lost ground quickly. Then the other hyena came at him from the side and he had to let go of the first one in order not to be bitten to death by the second.

All this happened within a few seconds. And while the wolf charged at the vulture, Krieg charged at her as well and when she lifted off, the horse unfolded his wings and lifted off into the air also. The vulture gained height fast whereas Krieg had to work for his momentum at first. But then he was up and Joshua saw him gaining on her as they flew ever higher until Joshua could barely make out who was who. And then their battle in the air began.

Joshua tried to get closer to Wind but the spiders surrounded him within seconds of the vulture's lifting off the ground. He had very little room to move and could do nothing but stare back into their dead eyes that were watching him vigilantly. They were about his height and a single one of them could easily kill him in an instant. There was nothing for him to do but to wait. He witnessed the wolf fighting the hyenas. Grey gave them hell, but Joshua knew that his attacks were finite. At some point his strength would leave him. Then he could only jump into the water. They couldn't follow him but there was no place to stand inside the round opening. It was a crater with a sharp edge going straight down. One could either stand next to it or swim in it. There was nowhere else to go.

Joshua could see the dark outline of the dragon on the other side of the spider's web. His body seemed to move and his contours changed and Joshua realized that he was covered with spiders that moved on top of him. His neck feathers stood up at the thought of it.

Joshua tried to communicate with the wolf but he was so focused on surviving the fight against the hyenas, he was not listening at all. Grey looked at him once and Joshua saw the exhaustion in his eyes. At some point he would have to give up. Joshua felt helpless and once began to fly over to him but a single shot of the sticky spider's web flew toward him immediately, missing him only by a few inches. It was a clear warning not to move. And then it happened. The wolf had just countered yet another attack from one of the hyenas and for a moment he stood, shaking, blood smears all over his coat, saliva dripping from his snout and near complete exhaustion. He had nothing left in him.

"I'm sorry, Joshua," he thought when he lowered his head, a sign that he was defeated. The hyenas closed in on him and Joshua knew that the wolf didn't have it in him to defend himself any longer. At that moment Krieg came crashing down, landing half on his legs and half on his side, tumbling several times, sliding on the harsh ground and ending up close to the Pegasus. He lay there completely still.

"Krieg!" Joshua tried to get closer but couldn't. "Krieg, are you alright?" He asked. There was no answer. Not a sound, a thought, or even the slightest movement from the horse. He might as well have been dead.

"Watch out, Joshua!" Grey's thoughts reached him at the same time as the vulture came swooping down and grabbed him. She lifted him up, digging her powerful talons into his flesh. She looked at him while she rose into the air.

"You have lost, Joshua Aylong and now you belong to me." With that she dropped him. He was at least fifteen yards up in the air and fell straight down. A few weak flaps from his wings slowed his fall somewhat but when he hit the ground it felt as if his body broke into a thousand pieces. He tumbled several times over and over until he came to a stop. The world spun around him. He could not focus his eyes on a single point. Sickness rose up in him and he knew that something was broken inside him. He tried to lift his head but couldn't move. The spiders had cleared out of the immediate area and he had a straight line of sight to Grey and the horse. Despite the pain he felt everywhere in his body it was his heart that hurt the most when he looked at them. And then he felt the end of all things descending upon them when the vulture landed next to him.

There was one question left in Joshua. To make him understand. To make him grasp what had happened to him, to his friends. There was a dream once. A dream of three feathers on a blackened stone. Why he searched for them he still could not say. But he did and it had cost him everything, and not only to himself, but also to his companions. The ones that were closest to him had suffered the most. Too high a price for a dream, he thought. Better end it now. But he had to ask the question. It was his curiosity that won over his fear at that moment. So he turned his head and looked straight at the vulture. It was as if he looked into an abyss of unimaginable horror.

"Why?" He asked, despite it all.

The vulture cocked her head as if she couldn't believe that he could ask this question.

"Why? There is no why," she answered simply. "You opened the door and I stepped through it. And what happens from now on is on you. Your dream awoke me. You defeated the mirror labyrinth that was designed never to be defeated. It activated the light beacon connecting this world with another and from there with yet another and many more beyond that one. In time all of Hollow's Gate will awaken. And all of it will serve me, will feed and give strength to my legions. And when we have reached critical mass, I will send them through the beacon and into the other worlds and from there into the others beyond. And darkness will reign until the end of days."

Joshua was in shock. The revelation that he was the stone that started the landslide that lead to the extinction of... everything... was too much for him. He closed his eyes. For a moment, he heard the sliver of a melody.

"LOOK AT ME!" The vulture screamed in her thoughts. He did not dare not to follow her command. When he opened his eyes, her face was close to his. "You gave me life, Joshua. And now, through your death, this life will become eternal. And nothing will have the power to stop me." The vulture looked up, spreading her wings and letting out a cry as if to summon the heavens for her purpose alone. Joshua closed his eyes again. The melody was like a whisper that slowly gained momentum.

The vulture turned Joshua on his back and stepped onto both his wings, pinning him down. Her beak was lifted in the air ready to strike and take his life to gain hers forever. Deep inside him something stirred. Something made its way to the surface. Fluid motions, powerful jaws and legs, eyes penetrating his very soul. The lioness had awakened. And Joshua let her go free. He was no longer in the way. He stepped aside, opening an ancient door that was shut for all too long. She had answered his call and he saw her. Low to the ground she came toward him, an amalgam of speed, power and grace. And when Joshua opened his eyes, the vulture saw the face of the lioness in him. There was a moment of absolute terror in her—a terror she had not yet experienced. It hit her like a battering ram. She saw the lioness in Joshua's eyes and she knew she could not stand against her.

Joshua let out a rooster crow that echoed through the cave and beyond. And at that moment, the melody reached its crescendo.

"TURTLE!" The wolf's thoughts reached him the moment Alda broke through the surface of the water. Her massive body was suspended in the air for a moment. Joshua saw the vulture, still fighting the terrifying image of the lioness he had evoked in her. And for a split second, time slowed down. He saw the water cascading from the turtle's massive back. He saw the spiders react and try to move away from the crater. He saw Krieg lift his head. He saw the hyenas turn to flee and he saw Grey grab one of them at her throat, holding her down.

Then, with a deafening, cacophonic sound, the turtle slammed back into the water. The tidal wave swept over the edge flowing far into the cave, washing over Grey, Krieg and Wind, taking with it hundreds of spiders. The vulture lifted off into the air, screaming. Joshua was swept further into the cave where he was washed onto a small rock ledge. From there he watched the scene unfolding before him.

The water reached the dragon. It immediately began to disintegrate the spider's web. He shook his massive body and most of the spiders fell off his back. It wasn't that they died when the water reached them. It was more that something let go of their tortured bodies and whatever had stopped the process of decay now progressed with immense speed. Within seconds they were gone.

The dragon stood up. His wings unfolded in dark red leather like crimson. His fangs glistened in the dim light. His eyes were deep green like faceted emeralds. His dark blue scales moved like tiny waves when he let out a scream that filled the cave from one end to the other. Most of the spiders had climbed up the large pillars or fled deeper into the cave. The dragon breathed in. Joshua saw it and he knew instantly what was about to happen. He hoped it wouldn't reach him or the others. Then a liquid flame shot out of his mouth. It climbed up one of the pillars, incinerating everything in its path. The web the Pegasus was held in previously, burned up in seconds. The heat the flames generated was almost intolerable. Then it stopped. The smoldering air was filled with the smell of the carcasses of the spiders.

Joshua saw Krieg getting up and shaking himself. He saw Grey pulling what was left of the hyena into the crater. He saw Alda climbing out of the water and moving toward Wind. Now that the immediate danger seemed to be over, everyone's concern was for her. Joshua slowly walked over to them. His body hurt badly but he realized that the fear had left him. The image and presence of the lioness had obliterated it completely. He could still hear the cries of the vulture from far above them and he knew she wasn't finished yet but he also knew that they would have a few minutes of respite before she recovered. His fear of her was gone. She had lost all power over him.

They stood around Wind's body: Alda, humming a melody that sounded very much like a lullaby, her long neck extending outward and her head only a few feet away from Wind's; Grey, still shaking but slowly gaining back his posture; Krieg whose face was close to Wind's, nudged her gently with his nose. Her wounds had begun to heal. The water had washed away the infection and with it the deathly grip of the vulture on her body. Then she opened her eyes. They met Krieg's. For a moment she just looked at him.

"No limits," she whispered in her thoughts and even though it was meant for Krieg, they all heard it.

"No limits," Krieg thought back. And Joshua could feel the effect of Wind's thought warming the horse from the inside, easing his pain. His relief was visible. He seemed to relax suddenly as if a huge weight had been lifted from his shoulders. She was alive.

"How do you feel?" The wolf asked.

"I'm fine. I think. I can't remember most of what happened. Only bits and pieces." A shudder went through her at the memory of it. "How did you get here, Alda?" She asked.

"That, my dear, is a long story," Alda replied. "Let's just say, there are channels under the mountain that I had not explored before. This was one of them."

"But how did you find us?" Joshua asked.

"You mean, how did I find you? I didn't. Not directly. But I was... summoned. Summoned by the guardian of the mountain. The lioness herself summoned me. When she was released, I just followed her to you."

"You did not come too soon," Grey replied.

"I wish I would have been here earlier," Alda remarked. "Wind, I thought you dead and for that I am truly sorry."

"Alda, please. I do not know how to ever repay you," Wind answered.

"Neither of us does," Krieg added.

"There is no payment between friends," Alda's thoughts were accompanied by a different melody that seemed to come from all directions. And for a few seconds they stood quietly, listening to it. The beam of light illuminated them softly. Joshua looked from one to the other. He saw Grey's unwavering loyalty, Krieg's courage in the face of certain death, Wind's lightness and wisdom and Alda's joy spilling out of her with every note she sang. He realized at that moment that their circle of friendship was the greatest comfort he had ever experienced.

"You don't have much time." The dragon sat half in the shadows. His thoughts were like amber glowing in their minds. "Eternal life is within her grasp. She will not stop until she has taken it and made it her own. You must reach the cave of dreams far up below the ceiling. I will help you open its gate of ice but we must hurry."

"It is so nice to see you, Dragon-Of-The-Stone," Alda looked at the silhouette of the massive dragon in the shadows.

"And you as well," he answered. "My dreams were lightened whenever they touched yours."

"Do you all know each other down here?" Joshua asked.

The wolf smiled.

"We have been here for a while, my dear," Alda answered. "Over the last thousand years we have made some friends." A light and happy song accompanied her thoughts.

"We shall have more time later on, but I suggest we get our friends to where they need to go," the dragon added.

"Your wisdom has not suffered over the years," Alda added.

"My wisdom maybe, but my memory betrays me," the dragon thought back. "When I first fell asleep this cave was filled with light. When I awoke the only source of it was this small beam here."

"It will come to you. I am still missing many of my memories – good and bad ones." The turtle waved her head from one side to the other as if trying to bring them back that way somehow.

Joshua thought of something. At least he tried to. It escaped him each time he began to get closer to it. He still had trouble focusing but he knew he was missing something.

"The spiders will wait for us," Grey stated a mere fact.

"Yes. They will," the dragon answered. "That's why we have to be in the air when we get to them. We are almost at the end of the cave. There is a chimney at the furthest wall. We have to fly up in it to reach the entrance to the cave of dreams. I can open it for you once we are there."

"We can't all fly," Krieg added.

Joshua's thoughts kept going in circles. He was searching his mind for whatever it was he was missing.

"We don't have to," the dragon answered. "The red one can sit on Wind's back and it would be an honor for me to carry the great Grey of the Ice Forest to his destination."

"What about you?" Wind asked, looking at Alda.

"Our ways must part. For now," the turtle answered. "But not for long. We shall see each other again."

"I hope so. It is still my heart's desire to stand on the ancient ground of my childhood once again," Wind replied.

"So it shall be," the turtle answered.

Joshua's neck feathers stood up when the missing piece in the puzzle suddenly came to him.

"RUN!" He screamed in his thoughts.

Then all hell broke loose.

23. Dragon's Flight

oshua realized in a split second what the missing piece of information was. When the vulture stood over him and he was pinned to the floor, he saw the smallest movement far above her head. He had lost the thought at that moment, but he now remembered.

Suddenly there were patterns of light on the floor of the cave. Moving patterns. First, the light was sporadic. After a few seconds it covered more and more of the floor. They all looked up. It was as if death itself descended upon them from above. The spiders had let go of the massive web that was spun across a large part of the ceiling. They had been waiting in silence this whole time, blocking the light. When they fell on them, Joshua knew immediately that their purpose had now changed. They no longer came to escort them to the vulture. The spiders were now commanded to kill them, but leave him alive.

The dragon shot out a flame that instantly vaporized the first hundred in the air.

"We must take flight!" The dragon's thoughts reached them at the same time as the first spiders hit the ground. "Grey, come to me!" He thought to the wolf who didn't hesitate and jumped on the dragon's back.

"What about you!" Wind thought to the turtle.

"They can't harm me. But you must go, my dear. And take the red one with you," the turtle's thoughts were deafening, her music a cacophonic symphony of shrieking sounds.

"Come, Joshua!" Wind thought to him. He realized that she was still weak. Her first steps were uncertain and before he could reach her she was covered in spiders. Several of them landed next to him also. At that moment the vulture descended with a chilling scream.

"I will take care of her," Krieg's thought trailed off as he rose into the air and toward the vulture.

Joshua watched Wind fight the spiders but he knew it would only be a matter of moments before she would be paralyzed. He closed his eyes.

"Come to me," he thought. "I summon you."

And she came. Fast like a shadow, all fluidity and grace, the lioness came to him once more. From the depths of his being, she rose up and he stepped aside and let her take him. His rooster crow had the power and the fierceness of the lioness in it. When he flew toward the Pegasus the spiders fled. He landed on her back.

"Take me to the air, Wind!" He thought and the strength of the lioness swept over him and took the Pegasus as well. And she lifted off the ground and she flew, her wings carrying them up into the air. Joshua now saw the sea of spiders below. There were thousands upon thousands of them. The few that had escorted them through the cave were only a fraction of their total number. The vulture had, in fact, created an army.

Joshua saw the dragon lift off. Grey was crouched down on his back. The cave was now immersed in light that reached far and deep into it. Joshua saw Alda gliding back into the water. He felt the sting of her departure for a moment.

"Stay with me," the lioness commanded. And he did. He directed Wind toward the dragon. Dragon-Of-The-Stone greeted the lioness and for a moment Joshua felt a deep reverence coming from the dragon toward him.

"You did it, Joshua!" Grey thought to him.

"Not quite yet," Joshua answered. "We have to find Krieg. He cannot fight the vulture alone."

"Do not be concerned." The thoughts of the lioness filled his mind, brimming with strength and beauty. "Krieg is a powerful warrior. He will do what needs to be done. They are too far away and out of our reach."

"You must trust him, Joshua." Wind's thoughts came to him. "He has gone beyond his limitations and he must find the courage to believe this within himself.

Joshua thought about Krieg and he suddenly knew that he needed to do this on his own. "May the lioness lend you strength and walk beside you, my friend," he thought, hoping that his thoughts would reach him.

"I am with everyone who lets me abide in their hearts, red rooster of the Great Lake," the lioness answered and Joshua felt that she spoke for all beings that thought themselves small and puny and weak, reminding them of their strength and power and ability.

"We fly for the cave of dreams," Joshua thought. No. He commanded it. And the others followed.

* * *

They flew high above the sea of spiders and Joshua saw the magnificent beauty of the cave for the first time. The pillars weren't black. From up here they were a dark, earthy color that only appeared to be black from below. In the distance he saw what looked like a massive half-round chimney extending from the ground all the way up until it disappeared into the stone.

"The entrance to the chimney is close to the ground. We have to be careful. Let me go first." The dragon flew before them and began to descend. "It might be tight."

The closer they came the harder it seemed for Joshua to make out where the entrance to the chimney was. All he could see down there were spiders. They had made a barrier, closing off the entrance. As the ground came nearer, it looked more and more impenetrable.

"Brace yourself!" With only a hundred yards to go, Joshua saw the dragon breathe in and release a burst of fire engulfing the wall of spiders and instantly dispersing them. They broke away from the web they built across the entrance. The flames burned it up immediately. The four of them made it through the newly exposed opening and flew into the chimney.

"Stay away from the walls!" The dragon warned them.

Joshua wasn't sure of the reasoning behind the dragon's warning at first. Then he saw why. As they ascended inside the vast chimney the spiders crawled up inside the wall surrounding them. They held their speed. At least so far. He didn't know how long they would have to fly upward in order to reach the opening. He hoped it wouldn't be long.

It was an eerie flight. The sound of the dragon's and the Pegasus' wings was juxtaposed against the spiders' crawling feet, all of it echoing through the funnel like chimney. The higher they flew, the narrower the walls of the chimney became. At one point Joshua looked down. Far below them he saw the floor of the chimney blackened from the spider's bodies. A wave of dizziness washed over him and he decided to look up instead.

And there it was. Still high up, but visible nonetheless, Joshua saw the entrance to the cave, or what must have been the entrance at some point. Now there was a wall of ice.

"I will go first," the dragon answered Joshua's question before he could ask it. "I have one shot before I need to regenerate."

Joshua saw the powerful talons of the dragon above him. His pale blue scales shimmered in the light.

"This is it!" The dragon breathed in and stopped his upward motion, hovering before the door of ice that seemed impenetrable. Then fire shot out of his mouth, enveloping the entrance completely. At first, Joshua thought they had possibly confused the ice with stone because nothing seemed to happen. Then large pieces began to break loose and suddenly the ice changed into water. It flowed down the wall of the chimney, covering the spiders and releasing them instantly. The dragon's fire stopped. Wind landed on the ledge and without hesitation ran through the opening. The dragon hovered for a moment longer, then landed as well. Grey jumped off and followed Wind inside.

Joshua had hoped that the water would stop the spiders from coming through but he saw them already pouring into the opening. They climbed over each other, pushing each other down and into the water. The vulture demanded they not consider the bodies of their brethren and they had no choice but to follow. "Kill the Dragon. Kill the Pegasus and the wolf. Leave the rooster to me." That was her command. And they followed it blindly.

This cave was as vast as the previous one but without the pillars, and the ground was flat. There were areas of very fine, almost white sand interspersed with large plates of flat rock covered with silvery grey moss. For an instant Joshua remembered a sliver of the dream he had, back in the coop from what now seemed like a lifetime ago. And then Wind fell. She was about to take flight when she was hit by the sticky threads of the spiders. Several of them hit Grey as well. He fought it but in doing so wrapped himself more and more into it. The spiders descended upon the wolf, leaving him no chance. Joshua slid off Wind's back and landed on the floor. He saw that the dragon was already covered with hundreds of spiders. They began to spin their web around him with immense speed.

"No!" Joshua's thoughts screamed out into the cave. And his rooster crow gave the others hope and strength. They fought the spiders with a newfound ferocity and, for a moment, seemed to get the upper hand. But there were just too many of them. All Joshua could see was the dark bodies of the spiders. He flew up in the air trying to find something to use against them. Then the web hit him from several sides and he was pulled back to the ground. He hit it hard and the spiders began instantly to wrap him into a cocoon.

That was when the vulture flew through the opening. For an instant, Joshua's heart stopped. Was Krieg dead? Did he loose the battle against her and lay somewhere, body broken and dying? But then Joshua saw him charging through the opening, trampling the spiders underneath him. He gained speed and lifted off into the air. The vulture turned to face him.

"Do you think I really flee from you, war horse?" Her thoughts were shrill and piercing. "I let you pursue me to lead you here. So your friends can witness your final battle and mourn your death before I take them as well. You will make a fine general in my army once I have resurrected you. You will lead legions beyond legions of my soldiers and I will make you the mightiest horse of war that ever existed!"

With that she flew toward him, talons outstretched, her beak ready to penetrate Krieg's scull in mid air.

"Not this time!" Krieg thought and, just before the vulture reached him, he pulled back with his wings, stopping in mid air and moving his upper body backwards. When the vulture was about to dig her talons into his flesh, Krieg hit her with his hind legs. The blow stopped her in her tracks and for a moment she hung there, suspended in mid air, an expression of disbelief in her face. Then she fell to the ground like a stone. Krieg flew down and when she hit the floor he was there. She got up, disoriented for a moment. Krieg turned and hit her again with his hind legs. She flew through the air screaming, and landed only a few feet away from the opening. The spiders fled from under her.

"KILL HIM! She pushed her thoughts onto them, demanded them to obey her. But before they could react, Krieg turned again and delivered one more blow with his powerful hind legs. She landed inside the opening in a puddle of water.

Her cries filled the cave. Sheer terror stood in her one eye as Krieg held her down. The water began to dissolve her back and her wings, then her chest and head. Krieg let go of her. Joshua felt the terror going through the spiders at the same time as well. But when the vulture was gone, the terror left them in an instant and, for a moment, they remembered who they were and they remembered their brethren next to them and they lay down on the stone and died knowing where they belonged. Their bodies became light and transparent and one moment later they were gone. The cocoons disintegrated alongside them.

Joshua felt his strength leave him almost at once. He was exhausted far beyond his limits and sank to the ground. He saw the wolf collapse next to him and he saw Wind and Krieg leaning against each other before they lay down. He saw the dragon lower his head onto his front legs. Before sleep took him Joshua remembered that he had been here before, that he had walked this cave in his dreams. He had almost reached the end of his journey. When he looked at his companions however, he thought the price too high, the payment too steep. The sting of regret followed him into sleep and did not leave him even after he awoke.

* * *

"Joshua… Joshua…" Grey's thoughts gently brushed against him. "Joshua, wake up."

Joshua opened his eyes. The wolf stood over him, nudging him with his nose. Grey looked exhausted. He hadn't eaten in days. His fur had dried blood in it still—a reminder of his fights with the hyenas and sign of the sacrifices Grey had made on his behalf. After all that had happened Joshua thought he should be happy to be alive. But he felt despair. When he looked at Wind and Krieg who lay together across from him, he felt utter selfishness. Ashamed, he looked aside. Never did the thought of searching for a bunch of feathers somewhere inside a mountain seem more preposterous than at this moment. What had driven him to this? Why did he follow his dream—a dream that had caused pain to everyone involved, including himself?

He felt that something was not right with his body. There was a pain that seemed deeper than just surface scratches. "Will I be paying with my life for this?" He asked himself. At this moment he thought that if he were to die, it would be rightfully so.

"Nonsense," the wolf's thoughts, as usual, interrupted his own, attempting to break them up, stir them in a different direction.

"Not this time," Joshua thought back. "What I did was wrong. I should never have jumped out of the coop. You, Grey, would have been better off. So would everyone. Look at them. Look at you! Don't you see! The vulture came because of me and we all almost died and with us this world and all the many worlds beyond. What I did was completely irresponsible."

"You came for me," Wind's warmth enveloped him like a breeze in summer, lessened the pain he felt for an instant. "You knew what would happen and you came for me."

"I did not. It was Krieg who came for you," Joshua answered.

"And without you we would not have made it to her," Krieg replied.

"You would have been just fine. You would have been faster. Without me you wouldn't even be in this position in the first place."

"Yes. You are right, Joshua." Krieg stood up. "Without you I would be dead."

"And without you I would still be imprisoned inside the stone." Wind added. "You are too hard on yourself, Joshua. Let us help you."

"No. You can't. Besides, in my dream I walked this cave alone. There was nobody here except me."

"But don't you see?" Wind replied. "You dreamed of this alone but alone you would not have come here. We are here now. With you. We want you to find what you were looking for all this time—"

"BUT WHAT IF IT DOESN'T MEAN ANYTHING?" Joshua was surprised at his outburst. "What if... they are just three feathers on a piece of rock and I... we... did all this to see that it was worthless?" And here it was. The fear of the possible meaninglessness of his journey finally caught up with him. He had thought of this several times throughout their quest, but never did it appear so clearly within him. And now that it was out and known by his friends..., known by his friends that he was in all likelihood a fraud. What would they think? He felt like a child sending her friends on a treasure hunt knowing that there was nothing of value to find at the other end. Suddenly to go this final stretch of the journey seemed to require the most courage. Forget the vulture and all her evil intentions. To have this journey end in utter meaninglessness was more than Joshua could face.

"It will not have been meaningless." Grey looked at him. His blue eyes holding Joshua's within them. "But not finishing it would make it so. You have become my friend, Joshua. There can be no greater meaning than this. For either of us."

Once more the wolf's clear thoughts were not to be argued with, even though Joshua felt like tearing apart his logic and proving to him that he was wrong, that they all were wrong.

In the end, he had no choice. He needed to finish what he had started, however silly the outcome were to be. And so, he stood up, shook himself and began walking into the cave. Grey took the spot next to him. Krieg and Wind walked behind them and the dragon was last in line. After a few hours they heard the sound of water ahead and eventually they reached a river. It went to the left and to the right. It was wide and Joshua was just about to tell them that he had no idea in which direction to go when Alda's head peaked out from the current, accompanied by a melody that was reminiscent of a birdsong.

"Alda," Wind could not contain her joy. "I'm so happy you joined us."

"I wouldn't miss it for the world. Besides, it is far too important not to witness this," Alda exclaimed.

"Important? I don't even know which way to go!" Joshua replied. His mood had not lightened much for the last few hours.

"Follow the river. It will lead you to your destination," Alda answered.

"But in my dream I was walking on a straight line."

"Yes, that is true. But much has happened since then and you are not who you were when you began this journey. Follow me, my red friend. And do not despair."

And with that she pushed off and slowly the river took her downstream.

"Come, Joshua, fly on my back. No need for you to walk when I can carry you," Krieg told him. Joshua, still not certain what this was all for, jumped up on his back and sat down.

And so they travelled with the river slowly flowing next to them. Throughout it all Joshua was privy to the dragon communicating with Alda. They shared bits and pieces of the dreams they'd had during their long sleep. Joshua got glimpses of the worlds they had travelled and was astounded by the terrifying darkness of some and the magnificent beauty of others. His small life seemed utterly unimportant in comparison. He was fully aware of the dark clouds that occupied his mind since they had defeated the vulture. But he also knew that there was nothing he could do about it. There had been several moments throughout this journey when he could have given up. Now he couldn't understand why he didn't. It would have been so much easier. It would have spared him the moment of truth.

And then he saw it. The entrance to the smaller cave shone through the semi darkness of the one they were in. It was like a beacon pulling them toward it, making sure they arrived safely. Joshua felt his heart beat faster. He exchanged a glance with Grey who reassured him in his thoughts that he would not have to worry and that whatever they would find or not find, would not matter to him at all. Grey seemed tired. Beyond exhausted. Joshua didn't realize how skinny he had gotten until now. He was only fur and bones. Nothing like the powerful wolf he had first met.

"That is not me you are looking at. I am more than flesh and bones, my dear friend." The wolf looked at him for a moment. Joshua suddenly had the urge to fly down and walk next to him. And so he did. And until they reached the entrance to the cave, they walked quietly next to each other, enjoying each other's company.

24. Home

When they entered the cave they could not believe their eyes. They stood in awe looking at the domed ceiling, its soft glow illuminating the ground on which they stood. Joshua wondered how he could have forgotten this. He saw the patterns in the walls and ceiling—what looked like rivers and valleys and high plateaus. He saw a large circular indentation in the center of the ceiling and the aventurine patches that looked like pastures with threads of the bluest aventurine woven through them. He saw parts of a great lake and for a moment he thought his eyes betrayed him. When he looked closer he saw what seemed like a small house and another building next to it. And from there his eyes found the meadow and the forest beyond that.

"What is this?" He asked, not really expecting an answer.

"I see Hollow's Gate," Krieg answered.

"Where?" Joshua asked.

"Right here," Krieg looked at the center of the ceiling. And now Joshua saw it too. The circular indentation in the middle of the ceiling was a perfect miniature of Hollow's Gate. He saw the waterfall and he saw what must have been the mirror labyrinth.

"Look, the city of light ruins," Wind exclaimed.

And now Joshua could see the buildings that were made of light and the beacon in its center.

"How is this possible?" He thought.

"The Gate of Time," Dragon-Of-The-Stone answered.

"The Gate of Time?" Joshua replied.

"Yes. This cave, the ceiling in particular, is at the same height as the Gate of Time that spans across Hollow's Gate. It is a horizontal layer that you must have passed through when you came down. And because it is in between the flow of time above and below, it in itself is timeless. In it, past, present and future appear simultaneously. What you see, Joshua, is your own journey. From beginning to end."

As they went deeper into the cave they saw the Refuge and the Lake of Tears. Wind gasped briefly when she saw the hill with the spider holes. They followed the small river that flowed from the Lake of Tears to the Porte Des Lioness and from there deep into the mountain. They saw the massive head of the lioness in the cliff and beneath it they saw the pond where Broga had waited for them. They saw the cave where the vulture had almost killed Wind and they saw the dark gate into the mountain she used to bring the Pegasus inside. From there their eyes went through the mining town all the way to the dragon's lair. They saw the crater where Alda came out of the water and they saw the chimney that brought them up and into the large cave. From there they followed the aventurine thread from the ceiling down to the floor. And there it was.

The pillar of stone stood toward the furthermost wall of the cave. When Joshua saw it he thought it was small, nondescript, almost plain. But he could not deny the pull coming from it and he could not help but follow it until he stood before it. He wasn't able to see what lay on top as the pillar was about 4 feet high but he did see what was behind it and for the tiniest of moments it was as if he looked at himself. There was a full size sculpture of the lioness whose face he had seen in the Refuge and whose presence he had felt during the battle with the spiders and the vulture. He realized at that moment that however much he had tried to deny her presence ever since, he could not do that any longer. He had made room for her once before and he could not close the door to her anymore. He had to leave it open.

He turned around and faced his friends. He saw it in their eyes, saw in them what he could not see within himself. He saw the power and the strength and the grace of the lioness in each of them, reflected back at him. And through their reflection he could no longer deny it in himself. He welcomed her within him and she filled the void he left for her and he felt her strength arise in him. And suddenly he knew. Knew the purpose of his journey, knew where the feathers had lead him.

"Grey, my dear friend," he thought to the wolf. "I want you to look over here. Tell me what you see."

Joshua looked up and behind the sculpture of the lioness to her right. The ceiling showed deep green pastures intertwined with forests and aventurine threads of rivers. Grey looked at it for a while. And then he saw her. She stood on the edge of a creek drinking from it. Grey looked from her to Joshua as if he didn't believe what he saw.

"Look," Joshua thought to him. "Trust what you see."

The wolf looked up again and when he did, she saw him. She looked down at him.

"You have found me," her thoughts whispered. "You have found the ancient hunting grounds of our forefathers."

"Yes," Grey thought. "Yes I have."

Grey looked at Joshua. He could see in the wolf's eyes the gratitude he felt and, not far behind, the love that was between them.

"Go," Joshua thought to him. "Go and be with her."

Grey nodded ever so slightly. He looked from Wind to Krieg to Alda and the dragon and back to Joshua.

"Remember me," the wolf thought.

"You will never be forgotten," Joshua answered.

With that Grey laid down in front of him. Looking up onto the ceiling, he put his head down on the ground. His breathing began to slow down. And just before his eyes closed, the great gray wolf from the Ice Forest looked at Joshua one last time. And Joshua was sure he saw him smile. Then he left his earthly form and was gone. His body seemed small as it lay on the cold stone. It was but a remnant of a once great hunter, warrior, and friend. Joshua looked up at the ceiling. And he saw him. He saw as Grey charged full speed across the meadow, through underbrush and up a hill and toward the stream where she waited for him.

"Until we meet again," the wolf thought to Joshua.

"Until we meet again," Joshua thought back.

Then the wolf's thoughts trailed off and Grey and his long lost companion together disappeared into the forest and into the ancient hunting grounds beyond.

* * *

Joshua felt a sting in his chest when his friend disappeared. But he could not help be content for him at the same time. This was not what he had thought the outcome would be. But then again, he hadn't really known what to expect.

"He is at peace now," Krieg thought to him. "A peace that had eluded him for a long time."

"How about you, Krieg?" Joshua asked. He didn't really know why he asked. "Are you at peace?"

"I think I am as close to it as I have ever been in my life," he answered.

There was a moment of silence.

"You can go further," Wind told him quietly. "Learning to fly was certainly not the end. Questioning your limitations was just the beginning. If you wish, I will show you how you can go further and then go further still."

"I would very much like that," Krieg answered. "But I know what you would like as well."

"What's that?" Wind asked.

"I want to accompany you to the place of your childhood and stand with you on the ground where you walked in ancient times."

"And I shall meet you there," Alda exclaimed.

"And I shall show you the way," Dragon-Of-The-Stone added.

"That's settled then," Joshua added.

"What about you?" Wind asked. Her thoughts played in a breeze that lay on summer fields.

They all looked at him. "What will you do?" Wind asked again.

Joshua realized that he hadn't thought of it. He had also completely forgotten all about the feathers.

"I'm not sure. But first things first," he answered and flew up onto the stone pillar. When he landed, he was very surprised to see that there were only two feathers. He was certain in his dream he had seen three.

"There are only two. I don't understand. Why are there only two feathers? Where is the third?" He must have looked very confused at that moment.

The dragon stepped forward slightly, lowering his head to Joshua's level.

"They awaken usually either toward the end or at the beginning of each age. For on either of the two outermost points on the pendulum there is a searcher and one that will most likely swing it back in the other direction and toward the balance point. There have been two before you, Joshua. Two searchers. Two feathers. Two civilizations. The first came at the outset of one. He set things in motion. The second came at the end when the path became so clouded, so split up, divided and split up again that the right way was no longer easily distinguishable from the rest. She was the second searcher reversing the direction completely and by doing so ending what had been."

"The sky people. Was she one of them?" Joshua had trouble following the dragon's thoughts. The ideas were too vast for him to let them in completely.

"We do not know. I was very young when it happened and I have no recollection of what had occurred," the dragon answered. "But I do know that you are the third. The searcher who stands at the dawn of a third civilization."

Joshua was stunned. He had so many questions.

"How?" Was all he could ask.

"It is very simple, really. The dream is the beginning. Many have had it, Joshua. Few have answered it. But in the last thousand years you were the only one who came this far, who actually followed it through and all the way to the end."

"But I didn't do it myself," Joshua thought. "I had... help."

"Yes, you did and mighty it was. The companions the dreamer chooses says much about who he is. Think of the wolf and the war horse. Better friends no one can have."

"Yes." Joshua thought, looking at Krieg. "What about the lioness?"

"What about her?" The dragon answered.

"Who was she?"

All was quiet. Joshua saw his reflection in the green irises of the large dragon. Could it be? Was this even possible? No, probably not. But after he had thought it out, Joshua couldn't help but realize the truth in what he had thought impossible at first.

"She was the second searcher."

"In a way," the dragon answered.

"The second searcher was a lioness?" Joshua asked.

"Yes and no. She spoke to you through her. That was the only way you could accept her help."

Joshua thought about this for a moment.

"What happens now?" He asked.

"That is completely up to you. You decide where you wish to go from here," the dragon answered.

"Can I meet her?" He asked.

"You have met her, Joshua. You have accepted her power and her strength within you. What else is there to meet?"

Joshua thought for a second that the wolf had spoken. The logic of it was so like him. He looked around the cave. He saw the sculpture of the lioness and from her he looked up at the ceiling. There was an opening right above where he stood on the stone pillar. The light was too bright and he couldn't see where it was going.

"What's up there?" He asked.

"Why don't you find out," the dragon answered. And with that, he stepped back again. Joshua looked at Wind and from her to Krieg and from him to Alda.

"Am I going to die?" He wasn't really sure where this question came from.

For a moment all was quiet.

"You can't," Wind answered. "Not anymore.

"And what about my limitations?" He asked.

Wind smiled in her thoughts. "You left them behind when you flew out of the pen. And from then on you have gone far beyond them."

Joshua looked at her, feeling her embrace and her warmth spilling out toward him and enveloping him completely. He felt the love he had felt when he first saw the feathers in his dream. Love for the Pegasus, Krieg, the turtle and the dragon. And for Grey who had not left his heart since he had gone to be with his companion. And he felt it for the vulture and the spiders and all the beasts of Hollow's Gate and beyond it far up to the surface. He felt it for his hens and their chicks and even for the farmer. Hadn't he given him the place from where he could begin his journey?

"I will never forget any of you," he thought. "I wish everyone could experience, at least once in their lifetime, what it means to have friends like you."

"The honor is all ours," Krieg answered.

Joshua looked from one to the other, then up again toward the ceiling. For a moment he thought about what would come next. But as he didn't know it, it didn't make much sense to think about it further. He felt lighter suddenly. The pain that he'd had since the vulture dropped him was gone. But he also felt lighter in his heart. As if a burden was lifted from him. He felt suddenly that he could breathe deeply.

And with that thought he nodded slightly to the others and he opened his wings and flew up toward the light in the ceiling. And for a while the others still saw him, flying upward until he became just a silhouette that eventually disappeared into the light.

They stood in silence for a while. Then they saw a single feather float down from the ceiling and land on the stone pillar next to the other two. It was red.

The End

May your heart sing with Alda
May it soar with the eagles high above
Take flight with Wind and Krieg
With the strength of the lioness
And may it be true like the wolfs'
May you dream deep and wide and vast like
Dragon-On-The-Stone
And may your dreams reach the stars and beyond
And may you have friends such as Joshua had
Always

25. Epilogue

ear friend,

As it is with many stories, the end of one is but the beginning of another. Just like the pendulum that stops at its tipping point only to swing in the other direction once more. There was one moment in my story in particular that has significance for what is to come. It was the moment during the ordeal inside the Labyrinth of Mirrors when I realized the depth of the love I shared with my beloved wolf. That moment has, like a pebble starting a landslide, set in motion a series of events culminating in the re-activation of the beacon—the ancient means of transportation between the worlds. And that, in turn, has re-awakened a whole civilization on the other end of the galaxy. I did not know this at the time. But I do know it now. As it turns out, this— all of this—is much bigger than I had ever thought it would be. And what will happen next, I believe, will surprise you, will astound you, will make you realize that to leave one world and to enter another does not mean you lose the one you left. It will stay with you. And just as the lioness stayed with me, the friends you made on this journey will always be with you if you so wish. That much I know.

We have not reached the end of our journey together yet. Keep your eyes and ears open. And watch your dreams. Always watch your dreams.

For now and until we meet again I remain very truly yours,

–Joshua

The Journey on the Map

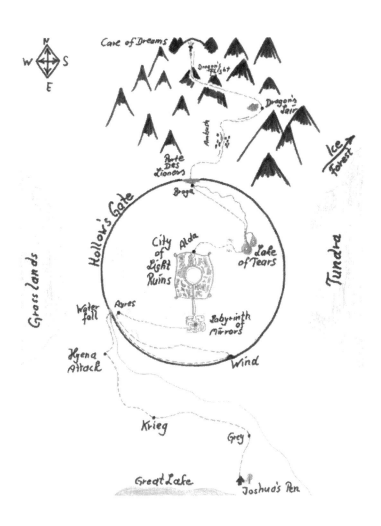

For what is to come and other updates, visit Joshua's blog and/or visit us on Facebook.

www.thethreefeathers.blogspot.com
www.facebook.com/TheThreeFeathers

Some of the locations in the story were inspired by the paintings of Hans-Werner Sahm.

www.alchemicalmage.com/HansWernerSahm/

The head of the lioness was inspired by a painting by Sheila Wright.

The amazing cover was done by Matt Maley.

www.mattmaley.com

Book Interior Design by Donnie Light

www.ebook76.com

About the Author

Born and raised in the beautiful Main River Valley in Germany, Stefan came to the U.S. in 1996 after attending a three-month long retreat in the Catskill Mountains. He studied psychology and creative writing at SUNY New Paltz. His dream has always been to become a writer. One morning he woke up and realized that he had become one. In his free time he likes to write poetry, shorts and screenplays, attend Karate lessons, read, go hiking and watch Lord Of The Rings. He knows this doesn't sound like much and there is a lot more to it but he thought he'd get at least some of it into this bio. He lives with his four girls—his long time girlfriend, her two daughters, and a black lab named Sophie (together with a bunny and an ever changing number of back yard chickens)—in the Hudson Valley, New York.

Even though he begins to get used to writing about himself in the third person he thinks it's kind of strange. He should probably stop now.

Made in the USA
Charleston, SC
02 November 2012